CH

THE CASE OF THE
FLYING DONKEY

CHRISTOPHER BUSH was born Charlie Christmas Bush in Norfolk in 1885. His father was a farm labourer and his mother a milliner. In the early years of his childhood he lived with his aunt and uncle in London before returning to Norfolk aged seven, later winning a scholarship to Thetford Grammar School.

As an adult, Bush worked as a schoolmaster for 27 years, pausing only to fight in World War One, until retiring aged 46 in 1931 to be a full-time novelist. His first novel featuring the eccentric Ludovic Travers was published in 1926, and was followed by 62 additional Travers mysteries. These are all to be republished by Dean Street Press.

Christopher Bush fought again in World War Two, and was elected a member of the prestigious Detection Club. He died in 1973.

CHRISTOPHER BUSH

THE CASE OF THE FLYING DONKEY

With an introduction
by Curtis Evans

DEAN STREET PRESS

Published by Dean Street Press 2018

Copyright © 1939 Christopher Bush

Introduction copyright © 2018 Curtis Evans

All Rights Reserved

First published in 1939 by Cassell & Co., Ltd.

Cover by DSP

ISBN 978 1 912574 07 0

www.deanstreetpress.co.uk

INTRODUCTION

IN JUNE 1939 and January 1940 respectively, Christopher
Bush published *The Case of the Flying Donkey* and *The Case
of the Climbing Rat*, both of them detective novels set in
France before the outbreak of the Second World War. Bush,
who was fluent in the French language and had visited France
many times, held the country and its people in great affection;
and it is hard not to see these two crime novels—both of which
reunite Bush's series amateur sleuth, Ludovic "Ludo" Travers,
with Inspector Laurin Gallois of the Sûreté Générale (the two
men had worked well together before in *The Case of the Three
Strange Faces*, published in 1933)--as a heartfelt tribute to a
nation that soon was to be mercilessly scourged by German
invasion and occupation. A little over two months after the
publication of *The Case of the Flying Donkey*, Germany would
infamously invade Poland, precipitating much of Europe into a
state of war. Less than four months after the publication of *The
Case of the Climbing Rat,* France herself would be overrun by
a seemingly unstoppable Nazi war machine, leading to the fall
of Paris on June 14 and the surrender of the country less than
two weeks later. Some 600,000 French people would be killed
in the Second World War, nearly two-thirds of them civilians.

For his part Christopher Bush, a veteran of the First World
War, at the dire advent of the second one went back into military
service on behalf of his nation. While France was collapsing
under the unbearable weight of the German blitzkrieg and
the British Expeditionary Force was desperately attempting
to extricate itself from seemingly certain doom at Dunkirk,
Bush was administering a prisoner-of-war and enemy alien
internment camp across the Channel in a Southampton suburb,
an experience the author would partially incorporate into his
next Ludo Travers detective novel, *The Case of the Murdered*

Major, which was published in 1941. Neither Christopher Bush nor his series sleuth would see France again for the duration of the war. Doubtlessly for Francophile detective fiction fans like Bush, the charming Gallic glimpses of a peacetime world provided in *The Case of the Flying Donkey* and *The Case of the Climbing Rat* brought back better and far less jaded days, when death could still be treated as a game.

The Case of the Flying Donkey (1939)

CHRISTOPHER BUSH dedicated *The Case of the Flying Donkey*, his first detective novel set entirely in France, to close contemporary Philip W. Cole (1884-1964), an accomplished painter and stained glass artist and principal of the School of Art in Hastings, Sussex, located about a dozen miles from where Bush resided at the village of Beckley with his companion, Marjorie Barclay. The next year Bush would dedicate his first wartime detective novel, *The Case of the Murdered Major*, to Scottish painter Josephine Haswell Miller, whom he may have met while stationed at Camp No. 22 (Pennylands), in Ayrshire, Scotland. These nearly back-to-back book dedications suggest the author's more than passing interest in painting, the central subject of his ingenious *The Case of the Flying Donkey*, which after the passage of six years felicitously reunites Bush's series sleuth Ludovic "Ludo" Travers with French police inspector Laurin Gallois, who in mental acuity if not in physical appearance might justifiably be dubbed the George Wharton of the Sûreté. (Scotland Yard's Superintendent Wharton, aka the "Old General" is, incidentally, absent from this tale.)

Three years before his marriage to Bernice Haire (this would be sometime around 1936), Ludo Travers on a visit to Paris fatefully purchased, on the advice of his friend Inspector Gallois ("lean, mournful, with the face of a dreamer and the long, sensitive fingers of a violinist virtuoso"), a small still life: a cozy kitchen scene which Ludo christens *Pot au Feu* after the French beef stew that is, according to chef Raymond Blanc, "the quintessence of French family cuisine . . . which honors the tables of the rich and poor alike." Ludo's prized picture, which to him symbolizes the "kitchens of all peasant France, and the peasantry which are France," was painted by Henri Larne, "a new, tremendous figure in French art," who drolly signs his name to his work with the image of a winged donkey (a play, Travers speculates, on the surname Larne, the French word for donkey being "l'âne"). After his marriage to Bernice, Ludo's proudly-displayed purchase was briskly banished by his unimpressed spouse to Ludo's den in their roomy flat at St. Martin's Chambers; yet although Ludo acceded to a wifely whim in this case, he never doubted for a moment that the 300 guineas purchase price for the picture was a steal-—though that price, Bush wryly observes, prudently "remained one of the secrets of his married life." (One has to wonder whether this amusing fictional domestic incident is actually drawn from the author's real life relationship with Marjorie Barclay.)

Three years later Ludo finds to his astonishment that it is this perceptive speculative purchase upon which he prides himself so much which pulls him into the investigation of yet another case of murder, this time in France, when a shady art dealer named Georges Braques, who in London evinced a great deal of interest in Travers' *Pot au Feu* and another Larne picture on exhibition at the Tate Gallery, is found knifed to death at his home in Paris. With Inspector Gallois and Gallois's boyish young protégé Charles Rabaud--"One day this little Charles becomes a someone," avows Gallois sentimentally to Ludo. "When I retire and devote myself to literature and art, there is someone who fills my shoes, as you say."--Travers tries to crack a complex case that seems somehow to involve masterworks painted by the great Monsieur Larne, as well as illicit picture-smuggling from war-ravaged Spain. Just what do Braque's partner, Cointeau, and Larne's brother, Pierre, know about the affair, not to mention that alluring and enigmatic artist's model Elise Deschamps?

Working together again after six years, Ludo and Gallois piece together a highly perplexing crime puzzle in time to allow Travers to salvage some of his Paris holiday with Bernice, who throughout the novel frets that she is doomed to live out her days with Ludo as a "detection widow." In the closing lines of the novel, Ludo promises Gallois--poignantly in the face of the awful fate which soon was to fall like lightning on France--that "the best is still left. The future . . . for us all."

Curtis Evans

TO

PHILIP

(PHILIP W. COLE, R.B.A.)

WITH GRATITUDE AND GOOD WISHES

AUTHOR'S NOTE

IT MAY BE objected by a purist that the translation of French conversations—between Frenchmen—are not the most perfect of colloquial English.

While such translations are by no means pidgin English, it was felt that too perfect a translation would destroy atmosphere and verisimilitude.

C. B.

CHAPTER I
MYSTERY OF A PICTURE DEALER

WHEN LUDOVIC TRAVERS came to look back upon the events that preceded the affair that was given the name of The Case of the Flying Donkey, they had an air of hurry and unreality, like events in a dream that arbitrarily change from place to place, with new characters and designs.

It was queer, when he came to look back at things, that he should, for instance, have ever purchased a picture by Henri Larne at all, even though the purchase had been an uncommonly lucky one. It was about three years before his marriage, when he had happened to be in Paris, that he had heard of Larne as a new, tremendous figure in French art; but the strangest thing of all was that the one who recommended to him the acquiring of some small work by the new genius was no other than his old friend Inspector Gallois of the Sûreté Générale.

Whenever Travers recalled Laurin Gallois, it was with a smile that had in it a kindly humour and a considerable affection. Gallois—lean, mournful, with the face of a dreamer and the long, sensitive fingers of a violinist virtuoso—would always protest with much shrugging of shoulders and a spreading of palms, that he had been ill-cast as an inspector of police when at heart he was really an artist.

It was on the advice of Gallois, then, that Travers made an appointment to see the famous painter at his studio, the Villa Claire, 40 rue Colignot. Henri Larne himself was a surprise. He was an older man than Travers expected—about forty, in fact—and looking as much unlike a painter as one could conceive. Then it turned out that his mother had been Irish, which accounted for his perfect English, and possibly—as Travers, the ready theorist, assumed— for his delightful charm of manner and his unconventionality.

Larne had few things on view, but Travers stayed for half an hour, talking about everything but art, which, for a painter, was also a queer enough thing. Out of the friendliness that immediately arose came a change in the nature of Travers's purchase, for whereas he had intended to try to obtain some quite minor work at a modest price, Larne himself expressed the wish that he should take a much more important piece—the picture which Travers immediately christened *Pot au Feu*. And Travers did buy it. Though he had no need to worry over money, he had intended to spend no more than fifty pounds. Now he had spent three hundred guineas, and he knew he had a bargain. And he knew, if pleasantly vaguely, something else: that in selling him that picture at so reasonable a price, Larne was giving a tangible expression of genuine friendship. It was not a large picture— roughly twenty inches by fourteen—but Gallois was ecstatic when he first cast eyes on it in Travers's room at the hotel. Those sad, soulful eyes lighted up and he raised hands to heaven.

"There," he said to Travers, "you have not a picture, my friend, but the—what you call?—the soul of France."

He said a whole lot more, and Travers was in agreement. The plate of steaming soup on that rough unpainted table was indeed somehow a whole nation, and what that nation was, what it felt and what it thought. In Victorian eyes the picture might be crude in colour, hopeless in drawing and childishly naive, and yet that table with its homely meal of soup and bread and wine was infinitely more than a mere still-life. In it one saw the kitchens of all peasant France, and the peasantry which are France: a peasantry of simplicity, patience, carefulness and homely dignity.

That picture was hung in Travers's study in the roomy flat at St. Martin's Chambers. When the Traverses returned from their honeymoon, Travers rather forgot the picture in the excitement of home-coming, and it was somewhat by chance that Bernice cast eyes on it. Travers caught her surveying it with an expression of very pained surprise. When he asked what she thought of it, he gathered that she thought it the kind of thing one would hand cheerfully to a rag-and-bone man in exchange for a pot-plant. Thereafter the picture remained in Travers's den, and the price he had paid for it remained one of the secrets of his married life.

Then the day arrived when Travers could afford to refer openly to his bargain. He opened his paper one February morning to see that the Tate Gallery was about to place on special and immediate exhibition a still-life by Henri Larne which had been bequeathed to it by the late Lord Draigne. Later that morning, when he was working in his den, he passed the paper to Bernice, finger on that announcement. Bernice failed to understand. Travers tactfully explained, and tried not to be triumphant.

"Then it's a valuable picture," Bernice said, bending on the *Pot au Feu* a much more friendly gaze.

"I don't think it would be dear at five hundred guineas," he told her. "The time should come when it's worth very much more."

"But, darling!"

"Well?"

"Isn't it wrong of us to have such a valuable picture here? Couldn't anyone steal it?"

"I doubt it," he said. "Larne isn't well enough known to the picture thieves. Also, I don't think more than two or three people know that I own it."

Bernice was peering carefully at the picture again, and pointing to a tiny painted something in the bottom right-hand corner.

"What is that queer-looking thing? It's almost like an animal."

"It *is* an animal," he said. "It's also the painter's signature, so to speak."

Bernice failed to follow.

"You remember Whistler's butterfly signature," he said. "Well, Larne puts what you might call a painted jackass to everything he paints, which, by the way, is very little."

"Yes, but why a donkey?"

"Larne," he said. "I know the pronunciation isn't the same, but think of your French."

She stared for a moment, then smiled.

"But, of course. *L'âne* is French for donkey. A funny name for anyone to have, don't you think?"

He smiled. "Perhaps it is. Still, we have people called Bull and Bullock, and Mutton, and Fox. Heaps of others, I expect, if we began to think of them."

But Bernice was looking at that tiny painted donkey again.

"What's that funny thing over its back?"

Travers polished his huge horn-rims, then took a quite unnecessary look for himself.

"It's a wing," he said. "It's what you might call a flying donkey. Its legs are stretched out to give the impression of flight."

"Yes, but why should it be flying?"

He shook his head. "I don't really know. Between ourselves, I rather think it's some expression of Gallic wit. It's a kind of ironical allusion to Pegasus, the flying horse. Sort of putting one's finger to one's nose."

Bernice nodded. "I see. Laughing at convention. But it's very crudely painted, don't you think?"

"Heaps of people don't take the trouble to write their signatures distinctly," he said. "But this isn't what you might call a picture of a flying donkey. It's just quick strokes with a brush to give a rough representation."

So much for the very preliminaries. A day or so later, however, Travers went to the Tate to inspect the Larne that was on exhibition, and he was there a minute or two after the Gallery opened, with a view to having the picture to himself. It was for the Van Gogh room that he made, but just as he was in the act of entering, he saw he was not the first of the morning's visitors to be interested in the new acquisition. There stood the picture on an easel in the middle of the room, but bending down before it in the closest of examinations was a man in dark clothes.

Travers withdrew again, and in a moment or two saw the head of the man appear round the opening. It was not Travers's way that he was looking but towards the farther door where the attendant usually stood. A quick, almost furtive glance, and the man was darting back to the picture again, but Travers had seen enough of his face to know that he was certainly a foreigner, and almost as certainly a Frenchman.

Travers, always one to strain at the leash when he scented anything of a mystery, shifted ground till he had both the man and the picture in view. The man was now bending down as if scrutinizing the bottom of the picture, and at the same time referring to a piece of paper he held in his hand. Then he looked suspiciously round again. Travers turned at the same time, and the man saw nothing but his back. But it seemed to be enough, for the man straightened himself, and then with an air of exaggerated interest began looking at the other pictures in the room. Travers moved on out of sight, and when he came back in a minute or two, the man had gone.

Travers, somewhat puzzled, took his own good look at the Larne. It was a picture much larger than his own, and, as usual, a domestic kind of still-life. The unusual part about it was that it had also a human figure, if only as a kind of background, for the black of the woman's dress set off the colour of the copper pan which she was polishing, and the other brass and copper that stood on the table by it. A somewhat earlier picture than his own, he thought, and more carefully painted than in Larne's latest manner. As for that foreigner and his strange secretiveness, Travers thought he knew just what had been happening. To photograph the pictures was forbidden without special permission, but the foreigner had been doing some surreptitious photographing for reasons of his own. Why he had been so interested in the lower half of the picture was probably something to do with light and focusing, with a view to getting in his photograph a clear reproduction of one essential thing—the signature of the flying donkey.

That same evening brought another surprise. A letter came by the last post from a man with whose name he was wholly unacquainted, a Georges Braque. A trade card was enclosed, and a glance at it showed that Braque was a picture dealer, in partnership with a Bernard Cointeau, their shop or office being in the Boulevard Bastide.

The letter was in English.

PENTLAND HOTEL,
February 13*th.*

DEAR SIR,

Mr. Blaine, the collector, informed me that you were in possession of a picture by Larne. I should esteem it a favour if I could inspect the picture at any time that was suitable for you, and if you will do me the honour of letting me know, I shall be greatly obliged. I shall be in London till the day after to-morrow.

With very many thanks,

Yours truly,
GEORGES BRAQUE.

He passed the letter across to Bernice, with: "This picture of ours seems to be coming into the limelight."

Bernice wondered how the French picture dealer could have known of its existence. Travers said that was easy to explain. Hereward Blaine, the famous connoisseur and art collector, had bought his Larne direct from the Salon, and therefore the dealer, Braque, knew very well where it was. When Braque saw the picture at Blaine's house, Blaine mentioned Travers's picture and that was that.

"What are you going to do about the letter?" Bernice asked.

"I'd rather like the dealer to see our picture," he said. "Sheer vanity, perhaps, but there we are."

"But why shouldn't you like people to admire your things?" Bernice said. "And when are you asking him to come?"

"In the morning, I think. Except, of course, that you're lunching out."

"It doesn't matter about me," Bernice said. "You can tell me afterwards what he says about the picture." She gave a rather tentative look. "You don't think he'll want to buy it?"

Travers laughed. "What you mean is, am I likely to sell it? But I don't think we ought to sell, at the moment. It's like realizing a first-class investment."

Travers usually did his thinking in the last few minutes before sleep, and that night he did happen to wonder if Braque could by any chance be the curious gentleman he had seen in that room at the Tate. Then he made up his mind that he would ring Hereward Blaine and get more information, and after breakfast the following morning he got hold of Blaine at his town house.

"I'm very glad you rang me up," Blaine said. "Has Monsieur Braque been to see you yet?"

"I've just sent a message to his hotel," Travers said, "and he's coming at midday—at least, so I expect."

"Well, there's something fishy," Blaine went on. "The only thing he seemed to be interested in about my picture was what I gave for it. Said he might have a client for it if I was ever prepared to sell."

"And how did he strike you personally?"

"Very specious. His English is pretty bad, by the way, but he had all the old clichés about art. Very little practical knowledge at all—I mean about the kind of things he saw here. Then he said that if I was in Paris in the near future, would I ring him up at his shop and he'd arrange for me to see some things he didn't show to the ordinary buyer." There was a chuckle over the phone. "I thought he was hinting at indecent postcards."

"Well, thanks very much," Travers said. "I shall see how he strikes me this morning."

"Just a minute," came Blaine's voice. "One thing I ought to tell you. I was very suspicious about the man because he struck me as trying to be very much what he wasn't, so I made enquiries in Paris. I got what I wanted this morning. This business of his is quite a third-rate one. You know what I mean. The kind of concern that does a fifty or hundred pound deal occasionally and thinks it's doing dam' well."

"Then what *is* this man Braque? A crook?"

Blaine chuckled. "There's still a law of libel. You see what you make of him for yourself."

It was a highly intrigued Travers who waited that morning for the arrival of Georges Braque, the man who was interested in the work of Henri Larne; the man who did a third-rate trade and was now mixing himself up with a branch of that trade which would involve the investing of thousands of pounds, and the delicate use of knowledge which, according to that shrewd judge, Hereward Blaine, he was very far from possessing.

"What's the game?" thought Travers to himself. "Is he trying to put fakes on the market? Faked Larnes, and is that why he's having a look at every Larne he can find? Or is he a kind of thieves' tout, and spying out the land ready for operations? Hardly that, though, or he wouldn't have given a genuine address. Or should he be given the benefit of the doubt? Is he, for instance, a small man who wants to get on in his own line, and is trying to branch out into something big? After all, every big dealer had to start in a small way."

But as soon as Travers clapped eyes on Georges Braque that morning, he knew him for the man at the Tate, even though that first real sight of him made it seem preposterous that he should ever have descended to the surreptitious. For Braque was a man of immense dignity—the dignity, one might say, of the perfect salesman or shopwalker. In age he was about forty, and in appearance aggressively French, with a face that was typical Third Empire, and bore a distinct resemblance to that of Napoleon the Third. But that last was before he removed his hat, for then his head was seen to be bald, except for patches above the ears, and that somehow increased his dignity and made him look much older than he was.

"Monsieur Travers?" he said, with a little bow from the waist.

Travers nodded genially. "And you're Monsieur Braque. Do sit down, won't you? And let me take your hat and coat."

Braque stood his ground and bowed again. "Monsieur, my English is very bad. You perhaps speak French—yes?"

"In a way, yes," smiled Travers. "But your letter was perfect English."

"I employ a—a—"

"Secretary?" suggested Travers.

"Ah, yes—a secretary."

The situation was eased at once. Braque took a fireside chair, and Travers, never one to suffer from false modesty, plunged into not at all bad French.

"You would like to see my picture at once?"

"If it is without disturbing you," Braque said.

Travers brought it in and stood it in what he thought the best available light. Braque rose and contemplated it, giving many a little nod and his fingers toying with his short imperial. Then at last he waved a hand and delivered judgment.

"You will pardon me, but a very good example. It is perhaps late?" His shrewd, heavy eyes were suddenly on Travers's face. "Three years ago or more?"

"It was just about three years ago when I bought it," Travers told him.

"It cost you a considerable sum? No?"

"That depends," Travers told him guilefully. "What's a lot of money to one, might be a mere trifling sum to another." He smiled enquiringly. "The whole point is this. Assuming I'm prepared to sell, what are you prepared to give?"

Braque gave a shrug of the shoulders.

"For myself I never buy. For a client, yes. If I have such a client, perhaps you would be prepared to sell?"

"Always assuming the price is right," smiled Travers.

Braque was suddenly looking up with a look of crafty challenge. "You would take four hundred pounds?"

Travers shook his head.

"You gave four hundred pounds for it perhaps— yes?"

"Perhaps," said Travers off-handedly.

There was an awkward silence, and Braque was the one to break it.

"You permit that I take the picture to the window? I would like to see it a little more closely."

He took the picture to the window that overlooked St. Martin's, and as the bulk of his body hid it from Travers's watchful gaze, it was impossible to see what special features were his main interest. But there was no funny business with a camera— Travers was sure enough about that—and in a couple of minutes he was bringing the picture back and replacing it with an exaggerated reverence.

"It is as good an example as I have seen," he said. "I congratulate you, monsieur, on its possession."

"You have seen a good deal of Larne's work?" Travers asked him.

"Not a great deal. He is not what you might call a prolific painter."

"You know our Tate Gallery?"

"Tate Gallery?" He seemed puzzled, and Travers could not keep back a quick look of surprise. Then he shrugged his shoulders and gave a deprecating smile. "A dealer is not interested in Galleries, monsieur. One does not buy from Galleries. One buys from people like yourself."

"I know," Travers said. "But if you're trying to see as much of Larne's work as possible, you ought to go to the Tate. There's a very fine example on exhibition at this very moment."

"Indeed?" There was something of gratitude in the look. "If I have time I will certainly go."

Then the heavy-lidded eyes were raised again.

"The Gallery, it buys this picture itself?"

"It was bequeathed to it by the late Lord Draigne."

"Ah, yes," he said, and nodded to himself. Then he began looking round for his hat, and Travers promptly got to his feet.

"Your Paris business is a pretty extensive one?" he asked politely.

Braque shrugged his shoulders. "We do not make much talk, monsieur, but we contrive to live. You yourself are in Paris often?"

"Not very often," Travers said. "But I shall be there in about ten days' time. My wife and I hope to spend a fortnight or so there."

Braque's face lighted up.

"Then you must certainly come to see me, monsieur." The eyes rose again, and they had a queerly repulsive suggestiveness. "There are things I have which I do not show to my ordinary clients, but to a private collector like yourself—yes."

"At the Boulevard Bastide?"

Braque shook his head. "At my own apartment. I am a bachelor, monsieur, and it is a whim of mine to surround myself with things that appeal to me myself." He was looking through his wallet for a card. "*Voilà,* monsieur: seventeen, rue Jourdoise, St. Sulpice. You know it perhaps?"

"I know my way to St. Sulpice well enough," Travers told him.

Braque's eyes rose once more, and his shrug of the shoulders was something of a cringe.

"Then without doubt I shall see you, monsieur. A little discretion is necessary, perhaps, not to mention to all the world that I have this private collection which I do not show my clients."

Two minutes, and Braque was gone. Travers came back to the room with the queer feeling that the ceremonial thanks of the French dealer were still echoing round its walls, and he had also that uneasy feeling, somewhat akin to shame, that comes after a contact with the disagreeable or loathsome.

That Braque was a slippery rascal he had no doubts, but what intrigued him now was the precise nature of his rascality. Was that house of his in St. Sulpice a private cinema or some such abode of filth that appealed to the vicious and abnormal? Or was it that he had amassed a collection of pornographic art which could not conceivably be shown to his ordinary clients?

"And yet that doesn't explain everything," said Travers to himself. "Why that interest in Larne's pictures? Larne never paints anything pornographic, at least as far as I know. Perhaps I might sound Gallois about that. And why did Braque lie about the Tate? If he saw Blaine's picture and mine, why should he conceal the fact that he saw the one at the Tate?"

But before the day had gone, Travers had found a theory that was partly satisfying. Braque had thought of the purchasers of Larne's pictures as being—should one say?—modern and eccentric. He was interviewing them, with Larne's name as a kind of introduction, with the real intention of inveigling them to that house of his. There doubtless they would be led into some devilishly devised indiscretion, after which would come the usual and highly profitable blackmail.

"In any case," said Travers to himself again, "there shouldn't be the slightest harm in talking the whole thing over with Gallois in confidence. And, to make sure that Gallois is still in Paris, I might do worse than write him a line at once."

One other precaution Travers took before he left for that short holiday, which was to take the *Pot au Feu* round to his bank for safe custody.

CHAPTER II
THE SECOND MYSTERY

ON THE MONDAY AFTERNOON the Traverses arrived at the Hotel Mirande, which lies within a stone's throw of Notre Dame. Travers had used that hotel in his bachelor days, and it had been a recommendation of the ubiquitous Gallois.

In the morning Bernice was to call on some old friends, and Travers was going to the Sûreté.

After the considerable deal she had been hearing about him, Bernice was very interested to know what Gallois was like.

"He's a remarkably able fellow," Travers said, "otherwise he wouldn't be where he is."

"What a man's description!" Bernice said scornfully. "What sort of a man is he? What does he look like?"

Travers smiled. "Well, he's six foot one and very good-looking in a way. His face is rather sallow and he has very soulful, expressive eyes. There's something rather Jewish about him and he always looks very mournful and tired. Most people would take him for under thirty, but he's certainly nearer forty. I think that's all, except that he has the most charming smile and manner. He doesn't even smile like other people, by the way. There's something very sad and sympathetic about it, as though he could look into the future and see you were going to have a remarkably trying time. Oh, and he has the most beautiful hands, of which he's rather proud. I always think he'd look best on a concert platform with a violin under his chin."

"Now I call that a lovely description," Bernice said. "Does he speak English well? I was wondering about asking him to dinner."

"I'm going to ask him," Travers told her. "When it will be I don't know. He's rather a busy man." He smiled. "As for his English, well, it's about the most fluent I've ever heard. What's more, he generally contrives to get remarkably near to the right word."

Gallois had a new room at the Sûreté, and as Travers's eyes first surveyed it, he knew it for a room of paradoxes that might have been specially designed for its occupant: tall and amply spaced, with no hampering of the thoughts of Gallois the artist and poet, and its walls close-packed with files and dossiers for Gallois the man of action.

He came almost shambling across as soon as the door opened, and his face bore a smile that had in it all the sorrows of humanity. His English was as fluent, and at times as unexpected, as ever.

"Ah, my friend, it is good to see you again."

"And you," Travers said. "And still not a day older."

Gallois shook his head. "It is not what one calls the appearance that counts. One exists, and that is all."

Travers smiled. "But you're looking extraordinarily well on it all?"

Gallois gave a mournful shrug of the shoulders. A hand waved repugnantly at the desk, the books and the files.

"One must surmount one's difficulties, I owe that much to myself. All this, and nothing else, and I am dead in a month. As it is, one mixes with it a certain delicacy and finesse. There is—if you will pardon—the handling of the policeman, and the handling of the artist."

"Exactly," said Travers. "And you, my friend, are an artist."

"A cigarette?" Gallois said. "And you will take coffee? Black coffee, is it not? Madame, your wife, she is well?"

"Very well," Travers said. "My letter must have been quite a surprise to you."

Gallois smiled sadly. Travers suddenly remembered that he had never yet heard him laugh.

"Here one learns to be surprised at nothing."

The disquisition was broken off by the entry of a youngish man in plain clothes. He was medium in height and build, and his slightly snub nose gave him a friendly look.

"Monsieur Travers, this is Charles, who commences to be a detective. Coffee, Charles, please. Black coffee."

"A pleasant-looking young fellow," remarked Travers.

"He is a young man of what you call promise," Gallois said. "For the moment I am keeping him, as you say, beneath my eye. And now, my friend, what is this mystery that you mentioned?"

"It's really to do with that picture of mine—the *Pot au Feu*."

"It has been stolen?"

"Oh, no," Travers said. "What it may be, I don't know."

He began his story and Gallois made never an interruption. But somehow he must have known when that story was nearing its end, for all at once he was writing something on a sheet of paper, and while Travers was still talking, he was again pushing the bell. There was something lethargically graceful about each movement of those long fingers.

"That's about all," ended Travers, and once more there was a tap at the door, and Charles came in. Gallois handed him the paper.

"At once, if you please."

The door closed on Charles, and Gallois swivelled round in his desk chair.

"A strange story, as you say. You permit that I repeat the address of this Georges Braque, to see if I have it correct. Rue Jourdoise, seventeen, was it not?"

"You remember that it's his private address and he particularly emphasized the fact?" Travers reminded him.

"But why not? A man of business, like this M. Braque, wishes naturally that his private address should be private."

"And what do you advise me to do?" asked Travers, rather puzzled at the indifferent way in which Gallois was taking things.

Gallois shrugged his shoulders. "For the moment—nothing. You have seen M. Larne?"

"Not yet," Travers said. "I tried to get hold of him last night, and couldn't, and then I did get him at his studio this morning. I'm seeing him this afternoon at three o'clock."

"That is excellent. You will tell your story to M. Larne, perhaps, and if you think necessary you will tell me what M. Larne will say. For my part, I think he will be interested, and annoyed. Not with you, my friend. With this M. Braque who pretends to know so much and knows so little. But we forget our coffee, which is doubtless already cold."

They began talking about things in general, and Gallois had something interesting to say about Travers's picture.

"I have often wondered," he said, "why it was that M. Larne sells you that picture for what was really so little money." He smiled disarmingly. "You, my friend, thought perhaps it was an expression of friendship, because his mother was English."

"Irish."

"You will pardon, but in some ways it is the same thing."

"Perhaps you're right. But why do you think he let me have it so cheaply?"

"Who knows?" Gallois shrugged his shoulders with a veritable despair. "Perhaps it was that he needs the money. M. Larne is a genius—"

He broke off as if suddenly seized with some profound idea. Then he leaned forward, his lean fingers feeling the air as if to find the words he wanted.

"M. Larne is the counterpart of myself. You permit that egoism, my friend, because it is also a profound truth. M. Larne is a genius, and there are those who have also said that I, Laurin Gallois, am a genius. But I cannot work unless I have the mood. Everything is trivial, and it stifles the brain, and then—*voilà*—the moment arrives. It is inspiration, perhaps, and it urges me, and I work. I make perhaps what one calls a grand success, and behold I am a genius. And M. Larne, what does he do? People say he paints very little, and, my friend, I tell you why. Like me he hates the trivialities. He awaits the grand moment, and then he is inspired. Four times a year it comes perhaps, or less, and each time he produces a work of genius."

"And the rest of the time he does—what?"

"Ah!" said Gallois, "there once more you have the resemblance. When I do not work, I have my interests. I write, perhaps, or I mix myself with men of intelligence. Women, food, gambling— those interest me not. But M. Larne, he is different because all geniuses are different. You perhaps understand?"

"I think I do," Travers said. "Larne lives a pretty gay life in his intervals of painting. He spends as fast as he earns, and when he sold me that picture, he happened to be hard up."

"Precisely. And you are not annoyed?"

Travers laughed. "My dear Gallois, why should I be? It does us all the good in the world to have the conceit knocked out of us. All the same, I think Larne is an extraordinarily good fellow, and I like him very much."

Gallois had to smile at that. "But it is agreed," he said. "All the world admires M. Larne, and were I of sufficient importance, I should like also that he should be my friend."

There was a tap at the door and Charles once more entered. Travers had had the idea that Gallois had been talking merely to mark time, and now there was some confirmation, for there was an unusual alertness about him when he had glanced at the slip of paper that was handed to him. The door closed again and he got to his feet. Travers rose too.

"And now, my friend, about this strange affair of yours. You wish still that I advise?"

"Most decidedly."

"Then you will see these pictures that M. Braque keeps at his private house."

"You mean, if they're indecent pictures?"

Gallois shrugged his shoulders. "You will see whatever it is that you are shown. There will be no danger, no blackmail—nothing at all. I also have my ideas about M. Braque."

"Just as you say," Travers told him. "And when am I to go?"

"For a day or so you will wait. If there is no communication from M. Braque, then you will go to his shop in the Boulevard Bastide, and say perhaps that you have forgotten his address. After that, one will see."

"That's clear enough," Travers said. "And I'll let you know what happens."

"All that you must inform us is when you go to that private address," Gallois said, and with a peculiar earnestness. "You see me, or you telephone, and you say, 'At such and such a time I call on M. Braque at his private house.' That is all, but it is important."

"Wait a minute," Travers said. "My wife and I both want you to dine with us. What about to-morrow night? We can decide on things then."

Gallois said he was enchanted. Seven o'clock at the Hotel Mirande, and if Braque had not got into touch with Travers by then, a definite course of action could be agreed on.

Half-way back to the hotel, Travers remembered something. He had not told Braque his Paris address, so how could the picture dealer get in touch with him? A telephone kiosk caught his eye and he was just about to ring up Gallois and mention the matter, when he saw that the kiosk was occupied. A Gallic shrug of the shoulders and Travers passed on. After all, it made no real difference, and he would in any case be seeing Gallois again the following night.

The rue Calignot has no reason to call itself a street at all. In England it would he labelled Private or Unadopted, to signify that the local council had no interest in the state of its surface, which was a matter for the owners of the property which fronted it.

In it you would scarcely think you were three minutes' walk from a Metro station, and only a couple of miles from St. Sulpice. To all appearances it is open country, so backed is it to the east by the trees that border the river, and by marsh and nursery gardens to the west. It has perhaps a dozen villas in all, each a separate property well shielded by trees from the observation of its neighbours. The Villa Claire, which was used as a studio and a Paris *pied-à-terre* by Henry Larne, had its own particular advantages. It was quiet, secluded, and yet accessible; it had a tiny cottage of its own which was occupied by the woman responsible for the care of the house, and almost opposite it was a road that led direct to the *route nationale* to Melun and the south-east.

Travers arrived promptly to time at the Villa Claire, and he was admitted by a man who was obviously not a servant. He was wearing a grey lounge suit and Travers seemed to detect in him some resemblance to Henri Larne.

"*Monsieur Travers?*" he said. "*Monsieur Larne vous attend.*"

"You speak English?" Travers asked him smilingly.

"An English very bad," he said haltingly. "My brother he speak very well—you think?"

"You are Mr. Larne's brother?"

"Yes," he said, and gave another little bow. There was something too deferential about him that Travers found uncomfortable. And apparently he was none too comfortable either, for he said no other word till the stairs were mounted and he was opening the studio door.

"You will find my brother here, I think."

He had evidently been thinking out that sentence all the way up the stairs, and now was about to bolt. But a voice called him.

"Un moment, Pierre."

It was Henri Larne, rising from his chair by the far window with a smile of welcome on his face. Travers thought he had aged considerably since he had seen him last. He had run slightly to fat and there was a puffiness that told of burning candles at both ends. But it was still the old likeable Larne, and the smile was as attractive as ever.

"Well, well," he said, and ran a quick eye over his guest. "Delighted to see you again, my dear fellow. You're looking remarkably well?"

"I'm feeling well," smiled Travers. "And you? You're browner than when I saw you last."

"I've just got back from the South," he said. "This is my half-brother, Pierre Larne. He acts as my secretary and general agent. *Tu pars toute de strife, Pierre?"*

"Oui, je pars," Pierre said, and smiled a somewhat awkward *an revoir* at Travers.

"Pierre is younger than myself, as you saw," Henri said. He listened for a moment, and there was the sound of the car in which his brother was evidently driving away. "And now may I make you some tea? Or is it too early?"

"A bit too early, I think," said Travers, and then shook his head. "It always puzzles me when you speak such perfect English. You look so French."

24 | CHRISTOPHER BUSH

"But I *am* French," smiled Larne.

"Perhaps I shouldn't have said I was puzzled. It's more like a pleasurable surprise." He shook his head again. "Everything is a pleasant surprise here. Everything so simple and direct. I know men without a tenth of your reputation who're riddled with affectation and hedged in with secretaries and the lord knows what. You don't mind my saying that?"

Larne took his arm affectionately. "My dear fellow, it's one of the best compliments I've ever been paid. Now sit down, and let's hear all about yourself."

"Heaven forbid!" said Travers. "But might I commit another impertinence?"

"Another?"

"Yes. I haven't come here to buy anything, but would you honour me by showing me anything you have?"

"The honour would be mine," said Larne, and gave an apologetic shrug of the shoulders. "Unfortunately there is nothing. Five minutes ago I could have shown you something I did— something you might have liked, but an American collector saw it at Nice and Pierre is just delivering it at his hotel." He shrugged his shoulders again. "Things to see? Yes, plenty. But only for me to see. There is nothing I would show to anybody else."

Travers had been casting an eye round that room. It was much as be bad remembered it: lofty, superbly lighted and sparsely furnished. A bare canvas, prepared with undercoating, stood on the large easel.

"But you are going to work," Travers said, nodding at the easel.

Larne smiled whimsically. "Am I? I wonder. You see, it's like this. I have another commission from that American collector, but his boat sails in two days. All I am waiting for is the urge to paint, and the idea. Without that, what should I produce? Something like a dozen and more things in that room there, that I wouldn't let a living soul see but myself."

"I know," said Travers. "That's always the problem with the creative artist."

Then out of the simple friendliness of that room, there came an idea.

"I wonder if I might ask you something?"

"Why not?" smiled Larne.

"It's something my wife and I were talking about when she first saw your picture. You remember— the *Pot au Feu*. One can understand the punning allusion in that signature of yours, but why do you make the donkey fly?"

"Why?" His lip dropped and the smile became something bitter and ironic. For a moment or two he said nothing, and his eyes were on some invisible something across the room. Then the smile changed to one of amusement, and he got to his feet.

"Come with me and I will show you what I have never shown to anyone else."

Behind the far curtain was a door, and he ushered Travers in. It seemed a kind of kitchen, and there was a dressing-table and a washstand, as if for the use of a model. A small stove too, and against the wall a score of canvases. On the wall was a solitary picture, and looking at it for the first time, Travers saw at once that it was a portrait—and almost certainly a self-portrait—of Larne as a much younger man.

"You recognize it?"

"Most certainly," said Travers.

"And what do you think of it?"

"I think it's good work." He smiled. "You want my honest opinion?"

"But, of course."

"Then it's good honest work, in the first class of its kind. But it's as far removed from your real work—your latest work as can be."

"Exactly." He was taking that portrait down and standing it face to the wall. "That was the kind of thing I did when I was a younger man, and it brought me nowhere. The critics ignored me and I was a nonentity. I left France and I travelled. Sometimes I was hungry and sometimes I almost starved. Then at last I came back. I painted a picture, and I was discovered to be a somebody. The donkey, my dear Travers, had suddenly taken wings."

Travers said nothing. Before the concentrated bitterness of that voice, nothing seemed apt but silence.

"I was sought out," Larne went on, "and they tried to make a lion of me. The critics fawned on me and tried to batten on me. I shook off the whole mob of them, and I lived my own way. To hell with their hypocrisy, and their cant and their jargon. My job is to paint, and I go my own way. If it takes me ultimately to the devil, the choice is my own."

He shook his head fiercely, and was silent for a moment or two. Then the shake of the head became somewhat puzzled and his hand went to Travers's arm.

"You will forgive me for talking like that. I oughtn't to have troubled you with my own affairs."

"The fault, if any, was mine," Travers told him. "But there's nothing to apologize for. I see your point of view and I more than sympathize with it."

Larne smiled, and all the bitterness went from his tone.

"Forget it, my dear Travers. As for these"—he waved at the canvases that stood with their faces to the wall—"these are my experiments. You would like to see one?"

He turned one round. Travers polished his glasses, and peered hard for a good minute at what he saw. Frankly, it was a chaos of crude colour, and nothing else except vague spherical forms that seemed to be receding into some immense distance.

"It's beyond me," he said. "What is it? An experiment in light?"

"Exactly," said Larne, and his smile had something impish in it as he turned the canvas round. "But you understand why I don't exhibit the—shall we say?—the experiments? Our friends the critics are not quite ready for them yet." He clicked his tongue. "Here am I talking all this nonsense and forgetting your tea. Do let me make you a cup."

"I'll sit here and watch you," Travers said. "There's something rather interesting I'd like to talk over with you."

So while Larne began preparing tea, Travers told him the tale of the man in the Tate. Larne seemed interested enough, but as soon as Travers came to names, he looked puzzled.

"Braque?" he said. "A picture dealer of the name of Braque? Never heard of him. What did he look like?"

Travers described him, and went on with the story.

"Most curious, as you say," was Larne's comment. "The man's obviously a swindler of some sort. If so, where's the swindle?"

"That's what I hoped you might know. As I said, I think it's some blackmail scheme."

"Yes, but why an interest in *my* pictures?" said Larne, "What's he thinking of doing? Putting fakes on the market? Absurd, my dear fellow. In the first place, I doubt if it could be done, and also everyone knows that my pictures never go through an agent's hands."

The tea was made, a box of *petit fours* was opened, and the tray was taken to the comfort of the studio fire. Larne took a sip at his tea, then put the cup down.

"I wonder if I might tell you something? Something that might possibly be connected with this man Braque?"

"Do" said Travers quickly.

"This is in strict confidence between ourselves, but about a month ago, in the South, I think someone tried to kill me."

Travers stared.

"I had business inland at a little place called Tesceau, and I was driving there in my car. The steering gear went wrong and we found afterwards it had been tampered with. It happened on a fairly safe piece of ground, but a couple of kilometres farther on I'd have dropped a sheer thousand metres or so."

"Good God! And you never had an idea who did it?"

"No idea at all. I didn't tell the police. Only the garage people and myself knew about it. But that isn't all. I arrived here a few days ago, and what do you think I discovered? Nothing had been taken, but somebody had hunted through every inch of this house."

Travers raised his eyebrows.

"There we are, then," Larne said. "Why should anybody want to murder me, and what the devil was there to interest anybody in this house?" He shrugged his shoulders. "As a matter of fact, there are small things of value that could have been sold anywhere, but nothing at all was taken."

Travers was slowly polishing his glasses. For once in his life he was barren of theory.

"It's a mystery, as you say. The only tangible thing seems to be this man Braque."

"One moment," said Larne. "Did you promise him you'd go round and see him?"

"Yes, I did."

Larne's eyes narrowed. "You're interested in this as much as I am. I wonder if you could sound him in any way and—well, you know what I mean. This business has been worrying me, and this man Braque does seem something tangible, as you said."

"You bet your life I shall find out everything I can," Travers told him. "Whatever happens, I'll let you know."

"That's enormously good of you," Larne said. "Normally I'd tolerate no outside interference with my affairs—the police, I mean—but you're quite different. One moment, though. I've thought of something. Could you possibly come here and see me to-morrow? I wouldn't trouble you, but—"

"What time?"

"Well, at five o'clock?"

"I'll be here," Travers said. Provided he was back at the hotel at six-thirty, he would be in ample time for Gallois.

"The idea's this," Larne said. "I have my own methods of finding things out. I'll do some enquiring to-morrow, and then we'll compare notes."

Ten minutes later, Travers rose to go. Dusk was in the sky, and Larne switched on the light at the head of the stairs.

"Something very satisfactory about a good fire and a bright light at this time of year," remarked Travers. "And now good-bye till to-morrow. Meanwhile, I hope you get an idea for your canvas."

"Yes," said Larne, and then was suddenly looking up. "Do you know, I think you've given me an idea?"

"You don't mean, for a picture?"

"I think so," Larne said. "There's an idea if only I can fill it in."

"Do tell me," Travers pleaded.

Larne shook his head. "It's too nebulous at the moment. Five o'clock to-morrow, and perhaps you'll see things."

CHAPTER III
SIX O'CLOCK IN THE
RUE JOURDOISE

THE TRAVERSES HAD ARRANGED a sensible, free-and-easy pro-gramme for that Paris holiday. Each had different ideas, tastes, and objects in view, and it was only when there was an overlap-ping that they would be in each other's company. Travers par-ticularly wanted a round of museums and antique shops, and—not unexpected in an unofficial expert of Scotland Yard—a cer-tain amount of time with Gallois and a study of Sûreté methods. Bernice had shopping chiefly in mind, and there were those old friends of hers, and, of course, a theatre and a concert or two.

The first overlapping was the Louvre, which Bernice shame-lessly confessed she had never visited. A long morning was spent there, and it was almost one o'clock when they returned to the hotel. Lunch had just begun when Travers was called to the phone. Gallois, he imagined it was, and when he heard the strange voice he thought it was someone at the Sûreté, passing on a message.

"It is M. Travers?"

"Yes."

"You permit that I talk in French?"

"Certainly," said Travers in that language. "Speak slowly and distinctly, if you don't mind. Who are you, by the way?"

"It is M. Braque, who called on you in London. A friend of mine happened to tell me where you are staying in Paris."

"Yes?"

"You are at liberty this afternoon?"

"Before half-past four or after half-past five," Travers told him. "What is it that you want?"

"You can see me at my private apartment at six o'clock?"

"Provided I am back at this hotel at half-past. That isn't much good to you, is it?"

"Monsieur, I shall detain you no more than five minutes," Braque said. Or that was what Travers thought he said. The phone was none too distinct, and it was none too easy in any ease listening to French over the phone.

"Do you mind repeating that? The phone isn't very good."

"One moment," Braque said, and there was the sound of the receiver being well shaken. Then: "Allo? That is better, is it not?"

"Much better," Travers said, though in fact Braque was audible and no more. "If I understood you, I am to see you at six o'clock ac your private address, and the interview will take no more than five minutes. What is it you want me to see?"

"It is something private and very important, which you will very much wish to see."

"And how shall I find my way there?"

"But, monsieur, it is so simple. You take a taxi, and *voilà!* The taxi can wait to take you back. There is a door which will be open and you mount the stairs and there is the other door."

"Very good," Travers said. "At six o'clock, rue Jourdoise, seventeen, St. Sulpice."

He rang off and stood for a moment thoughtfully by the phone. What puzzled him was, who had told Braque the name of the hotel where he was staying, and at once he began to think back to that interview in the flat. Yes, he had mentioned that he would be coming by train and not by car, and he had mentioned the date. Maybe Braque had taken the trouble to watch the arrival of boat trains at the Gare du Nord, and if so he was playing a game that he evidently considered would be well worth the candle.

"As soon as I get in that place of his this evening," said Travers to himself, "I shall insist on his telling me exactly how he knew my present whereabouts. I shall make it a condition of good faith, as it were. After lunch I will mention the matter to Gallois."

"Well, was it your Inspector?" asked Bernice when he came back to the table.

Travers, who had told her nothing of what he considered the dangerous side of the picture dealer, gave merely the facts, and as amusedly as he could.

"But you said he wasn't at all a nice man," said Bernice.

"Did I?" He laughed. "My dear, if honest men never had dealings with rascals, there'd be very little trade."

"Well, you must be careful," she said. "One hears such dreadful tales of horrible places in Paris and people disappearing."

He laughed again. "Now you're pulling my leg. I promise you I won't let myself be kidnapped. You're not going to get rid of me half as easily as all that. Besides, I may take Gallois round with me. He's a fanatic where pictures are concerned."

"Then you can both come straight on here," Bernice said. "You did tell him, didn't you, that it didn't matter about dressing?"

Bernice left soon after lunch, and Travers at once rang Gallois.

"It is you, my friend," Gallois said. "You have some news?"

"How did you know?"

"If it is about the dinner, then you speak in a different voice. Our friend has asked you to come and see him, is it not?"

"Yes," Travers said. "He rang me about an hour ago, and I've arranged to go at six o'clock."

"Good. That is what you wish, is it not? At six o'clock you see our friend, and—*voilà*—the mystery is not a mystery."

"Yes," said Travers lamely. "But I was wondering whether you'd like to come with me."

"Ah, my friend!" There was a world of regret in the voice. "Unhappily I am busy. Also our friend wishes it should be in confidence, is it not?" Then quickly: "You have not by chance a—what you call it?—an uneasiness? No?"

"I don't know that I'm any too happy about it," Travers said frankly.

"'That, my friend, is foolish," Gallois said reprovingly. "You have confidence in me? Yes? Then this afternoon you will go. There will be no danger, no blackmail. At half-past six I arrive at your hotel and you tell me everything. You have seen M. Larne?"

"Yesterday afternoon, as I told you. He was very puzzled. I am seeing him again this afternoon at five o'clock. He says he is making some enquiries of his own."

"That is what you call, sensible. And you will ask a question of M. Larne? If by chance he sell a picture in Spain?"

"A picture in Spain!" repeated the astonished Travers.

"That is so. If you find it difficult, you will pretend you hear he sell a picture very valuable to someone in Spain. This evening you tell me what he says. M. Larne, he is well?"

"Very well."

"I am glad," Gallois said fervently. "Were I of more importance, I would arrange so that I too become a friend of so great a man. Perhaps some time, if he do not consider it too great a liberty, you will arrange."

"I'd be delighted."

"You are more than amiable," Gallois said. "To know M. Larne would be the grand moment of my life. And now, my friend, that is all. *A ton hôtel a dix-huit heures et demi.*"

Once more it was a puzzled Travers who stood by the phone. He had rung up Gallois knowing that all his problems would be solved at once, and every uneasiness dismissed. Now he felt, if anything, more uneasy than ever. Why had Gallois pretended that it was vital for him to know the precise minute of the call on Braque if he was going to take the whole thing as trivial and commonplace? Had he discovered something that had made him change his outlook? And what was that business about Larne's having sold a picture to a Spanish client?

Travers shook his head, and then all at once his fingers were fidgeting nervously with his glasses— a trick of his when at a mental loss or on the edge of some astonishing discovery. He was glad he had not mentioned to Gallois that curious business of Braque's knowing the hotel, and for this reason. *It was probably Gallois himself who had given Braque that anonymous information.*

That was it, thought Travers. Gallois was more interested in Braque than he had cared to admit. He wanted that private interview to take place, and earlier than he had pretended, and he had therefore contrived to let Braque have the news that the Mr. Travers was staying at the Hotel Mirande. Rather theatrical that, on the part of Gallois, surely? And then Travers smiled. Surely the last epithets in the world to apply to a man of the devastating seriousness of Gallois, were 'theatrical' and 'flamboyant.' Artistic, that was the word, if not the *mot juste,* and was it not a Frenchman who had made the immortal remark that speech was given to us to conceal our thoughts?

It was on the stroke of five when Travers arrived at the Villa Claire, and he told his taxi-man to wait. Larne himself opened the door.

"My dear fellow," he began. "I'm terribly sorry but I shan't be able to spare more than a few minutes. But do come upstairs. My brother is away and I'm desperately busy."

"But would you rather I didn't stay at all?" Travers said at once.

"Perhaps I was exaggerating," Larne told him. "Besides, there's something I want to show you."

"But you're going to work!" exclaimed Travers as soon as he clapped eyes on the studio.

"That's right," Larne said. "Your mention of the light yesterday gave me an idea. There was something in my mind and what you said was an impetus. I'm painting that picture at once."

Travers stared. "But can one paint by artificial light?"

Larne smiled. "How did Michaelangelo paint the roof of the Sistine Chapel? You know the Riccardi Palace at Florence? Benozzo Gozzoli worked by rushlight when he did those marvellous frescoes. And—from the sublime to the ridiculous—what about my own experiments in colour?"

"You're right, of course," Travers said. "You must pardon a layman's ignorance."

"And look at this," Larne said.

He switched on the lights and Travers saw he was using green daylight bulbs.

"It certainly makes a difference," he had to admit.

Larne held his hand in the light for Travers to see the effect.

"It takes out a lot of the colour, as you see, but it has the same relative effect on my palette as on the subject."

"A still-life," Travers said. "But why the ancient chair?"

Larne explained the picture. It might be called either the Tired One or the Lazy One, and it was to show a servant who had fallen asleep while preparing the vegetables for a meal. She might be painted vaguely, and the high lights would be the turnips, onions, cabbage, and the potatoes which were already in position, and, as Travers saw from the canvas, lightly sketched in.

"I like the idea," Travers said. "You feel you're going to do something fine?"

"I know it," Larne said quietly. "I feel like a hungry man; a ravenous man, tripes rumbling, as Rabelais would say." His face was the face of a dreamer, lighting with joy, and his hands were making vague gestures of pleasure in the air.

Travers suddenly realized something. "But you have a model coming. I think I'll be going—

"No, no," Larne said. "She isn't due for five minutes yet."

"An oldish woman, is she?"

"Oh, no," Larne said, and smiled amusedly. "My idea is to get something—what shall I say?—something piquant, something ironic. I know what's in my mind." He shrugged his shoulders.

"But the model—except as a symbolic background is unimportant." His finger was making invisible lines on the canvas. "She creates a mass just there, and makes this balance. A curve like this, and this, and this."

He broke off with: "I expect I'm boring you, but the whole thing is this. I've told you the kind of man I am, and perhaps you know me just a little. What I get out of life is a series of ironic stimuluses. The donkey flies in his own way. When I rang up the Models' Club I told them to send me someone young and presentable. When she wears that black dress and sits in that chair—little cocotte that she probably is—there will be an irony, will there not?" He broke off as if he thought he heard the taxi, then shook his head.

"But I am forgetting. Have you any news about this man Braque?"

"I'm seeing him at six o'clock to-night; in other words, in three-quarters on an hour's time."

Larne's eyes opened wide.

"That's sooner than you expected, isn't it?"

"Perhaps yes," Travers said. "If I can get out of him why he's ostensibly so interested in your pictures, you can be sure I will. What about yourself? Did you manage to find out anything about him?"

"My brother made enquiries through an agent or two," Larne said. "And he thinks that Braque is trying to impress people with my name so as to gain their confidence for some other scheme of his own. By the way, I went round to that shop in the Boulevard Bastide this morning. Braque was not there, hut I saw the other partner, Cointeau." His lip drooped. "A little fat bourgeois who probably began life as a picture framer."

There was the toot of a taxi horn. Larne grimaced.

"She arrives. Don't move, my dear fellow, unless you're in a hurry."

"I'd love to see the preliminaries," Travers said. "If I ever write a book of reminiscences, this will be a big chapter."

Larne smiled reprovingly, and then was making his way down the stairs. Travers heard a woman's voice and what sounded like quite a petulant argument, and then the taxi was heard moving off again. Another minute and the model was entering the room, followed by Larne. Her eyes dwelt for only a moment on Travers, but she cast a long, level look round that studio.

"This is Elise Deschamps," Larne said to Travers, with a wave for the curt introduction.

She was a girl of rather more than the average height, handsome in a somewhat wary way, and with a look that was thoroughly self-possessed and, at the moment, distinctly petulant.

"You are going to work by artificial light?" she demanded.

"How else does one work at this hour?" Larne asked gently.

"How long?"

Larne shrugged his shoulders. "That I cannot say."

She shook her head annoyedly. "Already I have had two sittings, and except that they told me it was important, I would have refused." She shook her head again. "One hour and no more."

Larne bowed with an ironic cringe. "As you wish, *ma petite*. But you are different from every model I have used. Most considered it an honour to come to the studio of I, Henri Larne."

Her mouth gaped. "You are Henri Larne!"

"Yes." Another cringe. "I am Henri Larne."

She smiled foolishly. Larne's lip curled and his tone dramatically changed.

"You are fatigued perhaps? Well, you do not even have to sit. It will be a posture of repose. I will explain all that, and then I paint for an hour maybe, or two hours, or three. When at last I say I am finished, even if it is not till midnight, then we ring for a taxi and you go."

He was now at the far door and drawing back the curtain, and he had picked the black dress from the chair as he passed.

"You will dress here, and since you are fatigued, you will make some tea or chocolate for us both. After that we paint. Enter, if you please."

The curtain fell behind her, and he turned smilingly to Travers.

"Everything ready, as you see. You will ring me to-morrow, or come and see me?"

"One or the other," Travers said. "It depends on what my wife is doing." He smiled. "I rather think I shall come. I want to see the picture."

"Perhaps there will be little to see," Larne said, but there was a confidence in his tone. "But you will not obtrude my name with this man Braque? I do not like him to think his antics disturb me. Also, I do not want that kind of notoriety; I mean, if it is necessary to take some action."

"Trust me," Travers said. "I shall be tactful enough." His hand went out. "Good-bye, and good luck to the picture. Don't bother to come down. I can find my way out, and my taxi's waiting."

In the gathering dusk the river looked chilly and mournful and in the air was a mist that looked as if it might turn to a cold drizzle. As the taxi neared the Metro, Travers saw that it was not yet half-past five, and at a handy cafe he told the taxi-driver to stop. A note was handed over for the man to get himself a drink.

"How long from here to the rue Jourdoise?"

"That depends," the man said, but didn't add on what. "Five minutes, perhaps."

Over a Suze-citron, Travers began working out his approaches to Braque. Braque would begin the talking, but he would say: "I know nothing about you and you know nothing about me. It would put things on a much easier footing therefore if you told me the real reason why you are interested in the pictures of Henri Larne. If you refuse, then this interview is at an end." Bluff, perhaps, that might not work. If it did not, then one could always shift ground.

Then Travers remembered something that he had forgotten to do. In the excitement at the Villa Claire, he had not asked Larne about having sold a picture to a Spanish client as Gallois had specially asked. Still, the harm was not irreparable. One could always phone later, and it would be some sort of excuse to hear how the picture was progressing.

Lights were twinkling everywhere, but they seemed mournful lights in the drizzle that was now-falling. Travers's uneasiness returned. He had looked for the rue Jourdoise on the map and had gathered that it was a tiny backwater. Ill-lighted, he now thought, and in spite of his laughing at Bernice, he began to wonder if he had not been ill-advised. And he had quite a fairish sum of money on him.

Then his eye caught the clock. Ten to six, and with the realization something of the uneasiness went. The small reckoning was paid and he slowly made his way to the taxi. For a mile it hugged the river-bank, then turned sharp left, and he knew they were nearing St. Sulpice. There was a sudden gloom as they crawled through a narrow way between tall houses, then the taxi turned sharp left again. It crawled again for a moment or two, then stopped at the pavement.

Travers got out and quickly looked about him. An unsavoury quarter, he told himself, or was it that it was merely ill-lighted and unimportant?

"Monsieur, pardon, mais—"

Travers jumped. It was a poorly dressed man, collar buttoned to his ears and shoulders hunched against the cold drizzle. His moustache was bedraggled, but. there was something of respectability about him. But the taxi-driver's voice was coming in. A moment and there was the fierce squabble of voices. Perhaps they were talking some Paris slang, but Travers understood nothing, yet something serious seemed afoot.

"What is it?" he demanded of the taxi-driver.

The taxi-driver collapsed like a pricked balloon. It was nothing, he said; nothing at all. Merely a beggar.

Travers smiled relievedly. The beggar stood patiently by and there was a hurt in his gratitude as he took the small note that Travers gave him. Then he shuffled off in the dark and drizzle, while the taximan snarled something after him.

"Wait here and keep your engine running," Travers told him curtly.

"*Bien, m'sieur.*"

"If I am not here in ten minutes, come and find me."

"*Bien, m'sieur,*" said the taxi-driver, and settled unconcernedly into his corner.

Travers turned to the door, with the 17 plainly above it. It was ajar and he pushed it open, and saw at once the stairs, and the landing which was feebly lighted with a gas-jet. A last look back and he was mounting to the landing. In front of him was that other door that Braque had mentioned.

He tapped gently, waited, then tapped more distinctly. There was no sound from inside, and then he became aware of a chink of light that ran alongside the door. His hand went to the knob and the door opened of itself. A light was suddenly dazzling him and it was a moment or two before he could see into the room.

A step forward and his foot struck something. He looked down and saw at once that it was the body of a man: a sprawling man with head towards that door. Instinctively he stooped and turned the body till he clearly saw the face, though all the time he knew that the man was Braque.

Then he turned the body till he could see what kept it to that sprawling kind of rise, and as his finger touched the dead hand, he felt the warmth, and wondered if he were still alive. Then he saw the knife that stuck sideways in the ribs.

Travers got to his feet. His tongue licked nervously round his lips, and he was straining to listen. Then suddenly he was closing the door behind him and making a hurried way down those creaky steps. As he burst from the pavement door he collided with a man.

It was the beggar again. With a quick *"Pardon!"* Travers waved him aside and was making for the taxi-man. The beggar's hand was holding him back by the sleeve.

"M. Travers. What is there? What has happened?"

Travers halted.

"It is I—M. Charles. There is M. Gallois who approaches."

A shadow was on the pavement at Travers's feet, and the lean figure of Gallois loomed up through the misty drizzle.

CHAPTER IV
GALLOIS IS AFRAID

THE LONG THIN FINGERS of Gallois gently stroked the cheeks of the dead man. As they neared the chin, they almost caressed the short imperial, and then with a shake of the head he got to his feet. There seemed to Travers some strange malevolence about his smile.

"A quarter of an hour ago, or twenty minutes perhaps, he was alive. One cannot say therefore that it was you, my friend, who killed him?"

Travers smiled feebly. "There was no earthly reason why I should have killed him. Besides, I didn't arrive till five minutes ago."

Gallois clapped him amiably on the shoulder. "My friend, I amuse myself at your expense, which is in very bad taste. When one stuck the knife in Monsieur Braque, you were at the Café Blanquette. Also if one wishes to—what does one say?—acquire a courage to commit a murder, one does not drink a Suze. One fortifies one's self with brandy, perhaps, or whisky. But again I amuse myself. You observe, perhaps, something strange about the face of Monsieur Braque?"

Travers looked down again at the face of the dead man, and saw nothing unusual. Even that slight gape of the mouth did not take away the simple attitude of sleep.

"Perhaps I make an error," Gallois said mournfully, and once more knelt down and examined the body. From an inner room came the sound of Charles's voice, as if he were telephoning and it made a queer uneasy background, so that Travers suddenly felt a strange disquietude, and something of fear, like a man whose feet have unknowingly trodden the edge of a precipice in the inky dark, and who now sees the sheer depth to which he might have crashed.

There was something hampering, too, in the use of a strange tongue, and even in that English of Gallois, fluent and perfectly comprehensible though it was. And Gallois himself seemed different, with his reticences and that one sudden, almost challenging revelation that since leaving the Villa Claire, every movement of Ludovic Travers had been watched. Or was it safeguarded? And was this new Gallois merely Gallois the man of action?

A queer thought came to Travers then. Larne had been different that afternoon. He too had changed at the prospect of action, and had not Gallois claimed a spiritual affinity with Larne? Gallois was now the artist he had claimed to be; reticent because his brain was busy with the working out of things, just as Larne's had evolved a finished picture before a brush had touched the bare canvas.

Charles came in, and Travers remembered something.

"My wife," he said to Gallois. "Do you think I ought to let her know?"

"Ah, that dinner of which I was so expectant!" said Gallois, and raised his hands in misery.

"Madame, as you say, will be disquiet. You permit perhaps that I phone myself? Meanwhile, you perhaps write a note—yes? And it is sent by the taxi."

More men arrived, and a doctor among them. Measurements were taken and all the routine began with which Travers was familiar enough. The body was turned over on its back, and there was red on the bare boards of the floor and red on the handle of the knife. Gallois said something to Charles, who began a search of the pockets.

"*Un moment!*" said Gallois quickly. "You observe the pocket?"

it was the inner breast-pocket he meant, with the lining visible.

"Someone took something out in a hurry," Travers said, "It was probably snatched out, and the lining came out with it."

"That is as I see it," Gallois said, and felt the pocket for himself. Then he looked at the hip-pocket. Its button was undone and it too was empty.

There was nothing lethargic about the way he got to his feet, and the snapping of his orders. All Travers could gather was something about taking the body to another room, and the mention of the name Cointeau, and searching of some sort. There was a scurrying here and there, with Charles alone standing impassively by, as if he, too, had thoughts of his own. He also was curiously unlike a detective, Travers was thinking, with that snub nose of his and the friendly boyish face.

"And now, my friend," Gallois said, "you and I will seek the—what shall I say?—the explanation of things."

He drew back towards the door in the far corner, eyes everywhere about the room.

"This monsieur demands to see you, and there is something of particular importance he wish to show. Then, my friend, what is it he wish to show?"

"You know what other rooms there are?" asked Travers.

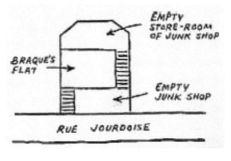

Gallois smiled. "There is no private cinema for the exhibition of what you call dirty films. Regard for a minute and I will show you all the house."

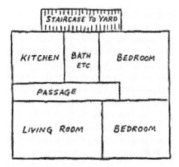

It was on paper that he meant, and in a minute Travers had the lie of the land.

It was Charles who drew the rough plan of the flat itself.

"That outer staircase is a kind of fire-escape?" Travers asked.

"That is so," Gallois said. "Once, perhaps, it was the only way of entering the flat. And now, the question that I asked. What was it that he was so insisting that you must see?"

Travers shook his head. "I haven't any idea, unless it was something he had in his pocket and which the murderer took away."

Gallois shrugged his shoulders and his spread palms remained a moment suspended in air.

"It is possible. But I put the question another way. What was it that you yourself expected to see?"

"Don't know. Ruling out—well, what we have ruled out—I should say some pictures. Possibly a pornographic picture."

Gallois nodded benignly. "And the murderer takes that too? It is more than possible."

He remained in thought for a moment, and Travers ran a quick eye round the room, with its cheap, if comfortable, easy chairs, its gas fire, and the small dining-table and chairs. Its only ornaments were the ornate vases on the mantelpiece, for its clock was also a cheap one for strict utility. But what looked like a brand-new cabinet gramophone stood in the corner.

"You remark something curious perhaps?" Gallois was saying.

"Yes," Travers said, "it doesn't strike me as a comfortable room. No, I don't mean that quite. It isn't a room that people have lived in a great deal."

"It has not what you call the English comfort," Gallois said, and nodded. Then he really saw the two pictures that hung on the west wall above a cheap and modern sideboard, and his face wrinkled with a kind of horror. Travers looked at them too, and made a wry face.

"My hat, what atrocities!"

One was a landscape: a view that never was on sea or land, with a flaring sunset to match. It was the kind of thing that only the departed junk-dealer below might have disposed of. The other was the head of a woman, and looked like the first effort of some art-school aspirant. The lip of Gallois curled at that affront to his artistic tastes.

"There is the kind of thing on which I would not even spit. We will see another room, if you please."

Outside the door was a passage, and there he halted.

"To me it is incomprehensible. If there is anything he wish indeed to show you, it is a picture. One who deals in pictures does not show you— what shall I say?—a table or a chair. You say perhaps he show you some papers—the papers the murderer take from his pockets—but I say, why do he wish to show you papers?"

"You permit?" said Charles. "The murderer perhaps takes the picture which should have been shown to M. Travers."

"It is the opinion of M. Travers that I wish," Gallois told him in French, "It is something that does not agree. To me there is nothing that agrees. Two and two make four, that is so, is it not? But here"—and he shrugged his shoulders expressively—"two and two make nothing at all."

He opened the door in front of him which led to a kitchen. Beyond its window could be seen a flicker of a torch where the men were doubtless searching for the prints of the murderer's feet. Beyond them twinkled the long row of lights from the boulevard.

Gallois came out to the passage again and opened the next door, which was that of the bathroom, which had also a lavatory and a wash-basin. Above the basin was a glass shelf and on it was a dirty safety-razor and an uncleaned shaving-brush. Gallois had a good look at them, and nodded.

"Here perhaps is one small two and two which make also a little four," he said, and looked at Travers enquiringly.

Travers shook his head. Gallois explained.

"The razor and the brush are not of this morning, you observe that? It is last night that he shave. He is lazy, perhaps, and he shave always at night, to save time, as you say. I also know that when I feel his face. But that is strange, is it not? He ask to see you, which is a favour. To him you are rich, and a client, and he wish to make the good impression. And yet he do not shave!"

He came out to the passage once more, and opened the door of the room to his right. It was Braque's bedroom, and the bed had not been made. A chest of drawers stood by the single bed, and one drawer was slightly open. Gallois was across at once. The contents of that drawer were higgledy-piggledy, and it was the only one that contained papers. The others had merely clothes. At the same time Travers noticed the telephone standing on the bedside table, and something struck him at once. "If he wanted everything so private, about this being his private address, why was there a telephone?"

"The telephone is also what you call private," Gallois said. "It is a number that does not appear in the book. That is always permitted if one wishes. But you observe that one has searched this drawer. It is not in a drawer that one searches for pictures."

"Unless they were miniatures," said Travers quietly.

"Ah!" said Gallois, and stared. "There is something that I forget."

He waved at the drawer and said something to Charles in a French that was too quick for Travers to follow, then made his way to the remaining room. As soon as he ran his eyes round it, he was turning to Charles again.

"This is the surprise, then, of which you speak."

That room was a mass of new furniture, not properly un-packed and none of it in place. It was showy furniture, and Travers also saw that new curtains had already been put up at the window.

"Ah!" said Gallois, as if delighted. "The good Braque was per-haps about to marry. You observe the bed, my friend. And the bride, perhaps, she already places the curtains. She have a taste for music also, perhaps. In the other room you doubtless observe the gramophone, which is of a newness veritably beautiful."

A label was still attached to one of the gilt chairs, and with his penknife he cut the string.

"It is necessary to telephone," he said to Charles. "Demand if you please, when one has delivered the furniture."

He was preparing to wait in that room, and he drew up two of the new chairs for himself and Travers.

"Sit, my friend," he said. "To-night, perhaps, we remain a long time on our legs. This afternoon you saw M. Larne?"

"I came straight from his studio to here," Travers said, and then smiled wryly. "Not quite straight, as you know."

"And you find a way to ask of M. Larne if he sell a picture to a client in Spain?"

"My hat, no!" said Travers. "Everything was so exciting that it went clean out of my head."

He explained about the picture and how the master was al-ready at work. Gallois seemed disappointed.

"I had wished that M. Larne should ask to see me himself. That would have been the introduction which for a long time I wish, and which I ask you as an honour to perhaps arrange. Now I am occupied. And yet I do not know. Perhaps M. Larne excuse if I telephone."

But there was evidently no hurry, and Travers mentioned that other curious happening which had just come back to him.

"Don't he annoyed with me, but I suppose you didn't by any chance—for private reasons—let Braque know my address here?"

Gallois looked astounded, then hurt.

"But, my friend, why should I do that thing? It is a confidence, and I do not tell confidences."

"I thought, you might have had special reasons of your own," Travers said. "After all, you have done a whole lot of things without letting me know. Having me followed here to-night, for instance."

Gallois got to his feet, and his smile was almost paternal.

"You forgive me, my friend. I do not wish that you should be alarmed. If there is no danger, then one laughs, is it not? But if there is danger, then one is prepared."

Travers grasped warmly the hand held out to his own.

"I have a regard for you, my friend," Gallois said, and his mournful eyes were dwelling on Travers with affection. "But who is it that also knows your hotel?"

"As far as I am concerned, only M. Larne."

"But M. Larne do not announce to all the world your address," said Gallois. "If someone tell your address, then it is not he."

Travers expounded his own theories, how that Braque might have been at the station that evening to await the arrival of the boat-train. Gallois agreed that the solution was a likely one, but it also showed that Braque had been even more anxious than suspected, to secure that interview with Travers.

Charles came back then. The furniture had been delivered a week ago, and no reason had been given for its purchase. Gallois merely shrugged his shoulders, and then said he would telephone Henri Larne.

"He will be annoyed, perhaps, that he is disturbed," he said to Travers. "Perhaps, my friend, you will do me the favour to explain."

"By all means," Travers said, and followed him out to the phone.

But in a minute or two Travers was aware that there was some difficulty. Gallois, who was trying to get the number, finally hung up. There was no answer, and apparently nobody in the studio at all! And with each word that he reported to Travers, the apprehension of Gallois seemed to be increasing.

"You're worried?" Travers said. "But there must be something wrong with the telephone itself."

Gallois shook his head. "It is not what you call worry. I am afraid." His hand rose, then fell. "It is for M. Larne that I am afraid."

His lean fingers closed round Travers's arm.

"Tell me, my friend. Who was it that was in the studio when you departed?"

"The brother wasn't there—"

"There is a brother?"

Travers explained about Pierre, Larne was there alone, he said, and the model.

"And you do not by chance know the name of this model?"

"Yes," Travers said. "Elise something or other. Elise Deschamps, that was it."

But Gallois and Charles were staring at each other.

"You are sure?" Gallois said.

"Perfectly sure," Travers told him. "Elise Deschamps, that was the name."

Gallois turned away, fingers feeling the air as if to clutch some thought that would bring relief to his mind. Then suddenly, dramatically, the hands fell. His voice was calm, though it could only have been excitement that made him still speak in English.

"It is foolish, perhaps, to have fear. There is something which I have forgotten. Charles, you will send a man—quick! He does nothing but observe what happens at the Villa Claire; who it is that comes and who goes. Ten minutes, perhaps, and I myself am there."

Charles appeared to have understood. Gallois turned to Travers. "My friend, it is necessary that you should accompany me, because you are a friend of M. Larne. But you will wish to see madame, your wife, and there are things I also must do. In ten minutes, then, I arrive at the door of your hotel."

Travers, glancing at the clock on the living-room mantelpiece, saw to his surprise that it was only a quarter to seven.

CHAPTER V
GALLOIS REVEALS

GALLOIS DROVE THE CAR and two of his men sat behind. There was no talking, for the wet paving-stones were dangerous, and Gallois kept his eyes on the road. The drizzle persisted and it was pitch-dark in that narrower road that led to the Villa Claire. Gallois, Travers already knew, must have come that way before, for he asked for no directions and it was near the Villa itself that he slowed down the car.

A man suddenly appeared in the light of the lamps, then disappeared again. Gallois stopped the car and disappeared also into the dark, for the lamps were now switched off. In two minutes he was back again.

"Nothing happens," he said to Travers. "Everything is dark, and there is no one who comes or goes."

He switched the sidelights on, gave an order to one of his men, then motioned Travers to follow him. As they turned into the gate of the Villa, the lights were switched off behind them, but Gallois moved unerringly in the dark towards the door.

He rang, but there was no sound of the bell. A moment's wait and he rang again. A third time, and another wait, and he stepped back from the door.

"There is no need to disquiet one's self," he said. "Show me, if you please, the window of the studio."

"All that next storey," Travers whispered. "It's too dark to see."

Gallois stopped and gathered a handful of gravel from the drive and threw it upwards. There was the sound as it hit the glass. He threw a second handful, hut before he could stoop for a third there was a sudden light. A curtain was drawn, the window was thrown up, and Larne's head appeared. There was a furious anger in his voice.

"Qu'est-ce qu'il y a?"

"It is I—Travers. Something has happened and I'd like to see you."

There was a moment's wait, and even then Larne's voice came churlishly.

"One minute and I'll be down."

He opened the door, still in his painting-smock.

"What is it?" he said curtly to Travers, making no move to let him in.

"It's Braque. When I went to see him, he was dead."

Larne shrugged his shoulders. "But, my dear Travers, that is no reason why I should be disturbed."

"Pardon, mon maître." Gallois stepped forward, and quickly introduced himself. Braque, he said, was indeed dead, but he was also murdered.

"Murdered? But when?"

"An hour ago, perhaps. You permit that we enter?"

Larne drew grudgingly back.

"Gentlemen, by all means enter," he said. "But I beg of you not to disturb me because someone is murdered. Whoever it is, it is of no consequence to me." His voice was rising and his hands were quivering. "I work, and it is important that I work."

Then his hands fell and the shrug of his shoulders was one of weariness, as if a whole world had conspired against him, and it was useless to protest.

"A quarter of an hour and I am at your service. Remain here, if you wish, or up above. It is the same to me."

"You are right," Gallois told him humbly in English. "My friend, M. Travers, he has already explained, and it is an intrusion that we make. You permit that we follow you upstairs?"

Larne led the way up and switched off the lights behind him. Just inside the door he placed chairs.

"Messieurs, I work. Silence, I beg of you."

And at once he was at work again. It was dark where the two sat but a greyish-green light flooded the small area of the table, and dark screens seemed to hold that light in place. The subject was now easy to discern. The maid lay back in an attitude of sleep. The knife lay on her lap and trailing down the black of the dress was the skin of the potato she had been peeling. On the table before her was a cabbage, and turnips and onions, and a copper dish in which were more potatoes.

Larne was sideways to where they sat, and already absorbed in his work. Greyish-green light came from his left and fell on the invisible canvas, and it was fascinating to watch his little paces backwards, his darting glances at the subject, and then the quick steps forward and the swift strokes and turns of this brush and that, and the sure dab of brush on palette.

Gallois whispered, lips at Travers's car.

"In the rue Jourdoise I was an imbecile. You comprehend now why it was that one did not answer the phone? And why the door-bell does not ring? One disconnects the bells in order not to be disturbed."

Travers whispered back.

"Everything is all right, then?"

Gallois shrugged his shoulders non-committally and slid back in his chair. A quarter of an hour went by, and another quarter of an hour, and almost a third before Larne stepped back and seemed to be making a final survey. Then he gave a nod or two and his voice came gently.

"*Alors, la petite, on peut partir.*"

At once she rose, stretched herself, then came sauntering across to the canvas.

"One has worked," she said, and in the laconic remark there was an immensity of praise.

"And you also," he said. "Now I call a taxi."

"You permit, perhaps." Gallois was suddenly with them. "There is no need to call a taxi. M. Travers and I depart almost at once, and my car is at the service of mademoiselle. What is the address where she wishes to go?"

"Rue Vagnolles," she said, and still seemed to be regarding him suspiciously.

"You will take a cup of tea?" Larne asked Travers.

Travers shook his head. Gallois also refused.

"I am myself fatigued," Larne told the model. "While you wait, make a pot of tea for yourself and me. For me, one cup of *thé Russe*. There is a lemon in the cupboard."

She disappeared behind the curtain, giving a last inquisitive look at Gallois, whose eyes were now on the picture.

"It is superb," he was saying, and even his English was a kind of compliment. *"Mon maître,* I have seen many of your pictures, but this is unique."

"M. Inspecteur is a critic?" Larne asked dryly.

"He is a fervent admirer of yours," cut in Travers. "You never knew it, but it was through him that I first came here, three years ago."

"A thousand pardons," Larne said, and he said it handsomely. "You will forgive that rudeness, and that other rudeness of a few minutes ago."

"It is we who committed the rudeness," Gallois said. "But, as you will know, I am the servant of the law. A man is murdered who has mixed himself with your affairs, and therefore we come to inform you of the matter. Now I have a request to make. You will do us the kindness to return with us and see this man who is dead? It is possible that you may recognize him."

"You speak English exceedingly well?" Larne said.

"I read enormously, as they say," Gallois explained. "English is a—what you say?"

"Hobby of yours?"

"That is it," Gallois said gratefully. "But you do not answer my question that you return with us."

"Why not?" said Larne amusedly. "It's a waste of time, but I have time now to lose. To-morrow I shall finish my work, but tonight I've done all I can do."

His cup of tea was brought in, and the model disappeared again behind her curtain. Larne drank standing. Gallois took advantage of the wait to look at the picture again, and it was he who indicated to Travers the tiny signature of the dying donkey that had already been painted in the bottom right-hand corner.

"And how long is it that you paint?" he said to Larne. "Two hours, and behold a masterpiece."

"M. Gallois isn't perhaps aware of the Whistler story," Travers smiled across at Larne.

"Whistler?" Gallois had pricked his ears. "Your English master, you mean?"

Travers told him the story of the action brought by the client of Whistler who claimed to have been grossly overcharged for a picture which had taken an hour or two of actual painting, but which, Whistler rightly claimed, had taken a lifetime of experience. Gallois, who had never heard the story, was delighted.

"That is a story which is—what do you say?—which hits a nail on the head. M. Larne, he paints for only two hours, but in reality it is a lifetime that he paints." He turned to Larne. "And now, monsieur, if you are ready we will depart. My men remain here on guard. There will be no need to close the house, unless you wish it, till your return, which shall also be in my car."

Elise Deschamps appeared, as pat as if she had been listening.

"Perhaps M. Travers will go down to the car with mademoiselle and make the arrangements," Gallois said. "Meanwhile, you permit, *mon maître,* that I use the telephone? It is not still disconnected?"

Larne chuckled at that. Then as the door closed on Travers and the model, the voice of Gallois changed.

"Quick, there is a question I must ask. You have worked with that woman before?"

"Never seen her before in my life," Larne said. "Why?"

"And how was it that she came here?"

Larne explained how he had rung the Models' Club, which was the rendezvous and bureau of Paris models, and had asked for anybody of her type to be sent.

"As you observe," he said, with a nod at the picture, "the figure to me is comparatively unimportant. To me it does not matter whom they send. But what is all the mystery?"

"There is no time to explain," Gallois said. "When we arrive at the rue Jourdoise, then you will see. You will need a coat and hat, and meanwhile, since you have permitted, I will use the telephone."

Larne shrugged his shoulders and waved across at the phone. A couple of minutes, and he was turning off the lights behind him, and he and Gallois made their way out of the now empty house.

The car circled and drew in at the rue Jourdoise the opposite way from that in which Travers's taxi had entered it. Gallois was driving, with Larne alongside him, and Travers sat at the back with the model, Elise. The car slowed, and then stopped. Larne got out and Gallois followed him through the same door. Men were surrounding the car. Elise stared frightenedly.

"Where are we? Why are we stopping here?"

It was Gallois who was opening the door and answering that question. It was in French, of course, that he spoke, and his tone had a kind of dry courtesy.

"We are all getting out. It will be necessary to wait here for a minute or two."

A look back at Travers and she got out. Two men closed in behind her. That empty junk-shop was now open and there was a light in it, and a gendarme stood at the door.

"You will be so good as to wait there," Gallois said to her. "I have business with M. Larne, and after that we will take you to the rue Vagnolles."

The drizzle and the mist must have made the surroundings unfamiliar, for it was only then she knew where she was. As the man's hand fell on her arm, she drew back. Then there was a shriek. A hand was clapped on her mouth, and the shop door closed on her.

"It is regrettable," said Gallois, "but what can one do? Now we go upstairs."

The body of Braque had been removed, and Charles was the only occupant of the room. Travers caught his eye, and he answered with a quick, friendly smile. Then he was his unobtrusive self again, and when he fell in behind Gallois, it was as if Gallois had once more become possessed of a shadow.

"This is the room of Braque," Gallois told Larne. "It is here that he was killed. But before we see him, I would ask a foolish question. You sell at some time, perhaps, a picture to a client in Spain?"

"In Spain?" He looked puzzled. "You mean, to a Spanish client?"

"That is it," Gallois said. "I did not make myself dear."

Larne shook his head. "Never to my certain knowledge. But that doesn't rule out the possibility that some Spaniard or other may not have come into possession of one of my pictures."

"Yes," said Gallois disappointingly. "One buys and one sells again, and that is no concern of your own. It is something of which I did not think. But the name Braque: that is unknown to you?"

Larne glanced at Travers. "I think I may say so. I've only known one person of that name in my life, and that was at an art school, twenty and more years ago."

"Braque may not be his real name," Travers said.

"His *dossier* is not yet complete," Gallois said. "But something else that seemed droll to M. Travers and myself. This Braque was a dealer in pictures. Why then in his own house does he place such atrocities on the walls?"

Larne had a look at the two pictures, then shrugged his shoulders amiably.

"But why call them atrocities?"

Gallois' lean jaw sagged. He could hardly believe his cars.

"The atrocities of to-day, my friend, are the masterpieces of to-morrow," Larne told him amusedly. Then a tone of irony crept in. "Manet, Van Gogh, Gauguin—even, if you permit—myself, commence with what one calls atrocities. It is a word therefore that I hesitate to use."

"In what you say there is a justice," admitted Gallois. "To be original is to be a fool—according to the fools."

Larne chuckled.

"My dear Travers, why is it that you never brought M. Gallois to see me before? I think that he and I are going to be friends."

"Mon maître, you are too amiable," Gallois told him delightedly. "But we must not talk of ourselves. This model who presents herself to you. This Elise Deschamps, as she calls herself. What would you say if I assured you that she was the mistress of Braque?"

"Mon dieu, non!"

"Mais, si. We commence enquiries and we learn many things. He is friendly with her, which is perhaps natural when she is a model and he is a dealer in pictures. There is the occasion, as you say, to meet each other and become acquainted. Then a few days ago he buys furniture for a bedroom, furniture very chic, very comfortable. You remark, too, the gramophone that he buys so that she pass the time when he is not here. But it is strange, is it not, that it should be she who comes to you this afternoon?"

"It's more than that," Larne said. "It's inexplicable. It must be some amazing coincidence."

Gallois raised a finger and his voice lowered impressively.

"One question I ask, and only one. You commence to work at half-past five. From then, till we arrive, she is beneath your eye?"

"The whole time," Larne said. "I never had my eyes off her." He remembered something. "Wait a moment." Then he shook his head.

"What was it that you thought?" Gallois asked him.

"It was nothing. You asked what happened *after* we began work, which would really be at just after half-past five. What I thought of was something that happened *before* we began. She was tired and made a cup of tea for herself and me. That's when I remembered she wasn't actually under my eye, but that was, as I said, before I began to work."

"I understand," said Gallois, already moving towards the far door. "One look at this Braque and in ten minutes you will be back at your studio."

"First I must eat," Larne said, "and so you see there will be no need to derange you and use your car. I shall dine at the Petite Musette, and then a taxi, and—*voilà.*"

Braque's body lay on the kitchen table, legs resting on the back of a chair. The doctor was at work on it when Gallois and his inevitable shadow, Charles, came into the room. Gallois merely waved a hand. Larne came close and looked down.

He shook his head and was turning away. Then he looked again. His hand went out and covered the short imperial. Then it covered the mouth too, and he was motionless while he looked. Then he turned away, shaking his head perplexedly.

"I don't see why you should believe me, but this is the Braque who was a student with me at the Academie Poussin. The Braque I mentioned to you just now."

All he could tell about Braque, and himself, was this. He had studied at the Poussin from 1914 to the end of 1915, and Braque had been a fellow-student. Braque's parents were supposed to be well off, and he was an idler. Then Larne served in the trenches till the Armistice, after which he decided not to return to the school, for his father had died and there was no money available. He had heard nothing of Braque, and in any case he had always been on bad terms with him at the school.

"But why should he become a dealer?" asked Gallois.

Larne smiled. "He had spent his money, perhaps. Also he was one who did not commence by painting atrocities. That was something at which he gradually arrived." He turned to Travers. "Was there ever a dealer who could also paint? Not in your experience or mine. Very well then. Everything is plain. When one cannot paint one can always become a dealer."

A mournful smile passed quickly over Gallois face, and then he was moving back to the door.

"For to-night, that is all. You stay long in Paris?"

Larne explained that he had left the South only because of the commission for the American collector.

"Then one does not see the picture again?" asked Gallois in consternation.

Larne said he might see it at any time up to four o'clock the following afternoon. It was a deeply gratified Gallois who showed him out of the room and ushered him all the way down to the pavement.

It was Charles to whom Gallois addressed himself when he came back.

"Everything is arranged?"

"Everything."

The eyes of Gallois narrowed. "Ensure, *mon petit,* that all is perfect. One mistake and there is something I should not bring myself to pardon."

Charles, imperturbable as ever, went out to the passage.

"A comedy is about to play itself," Gallois said to Travers. "But first we see this Elise Deschamps."

He made a signal at the outer door and in a minute she was being brought into the room. There was nothing hysterical about her now, and her look was watchful and sullen.

Gallois motioned her to a seat and he himself sat with arms resting on the table. His look was that of a father who is forced at last to appeal to—and reprimand—the daughter who is near to breaking his heart.

"Why was it that you shrieked?" he said. "We do not bring you here to do you harm."

There are many Englishmen who find it easier to follow the French of a woman than a man. Travers, who could get the gist of most conversations, found a quality in her voice, and—when she was excited— a speed that made her almost incomprehensible. He did gather that she had thought she was being kidnapped.

"But that is droll," said Gallois amusedly. "You are twenty-seven and a woman. One admits that you are good-looking, but it is not for that people are kidnapped. It is for ransom, and one does not expect a model to be a mine of that kind of gold. You have been a model—how long?"

The words came in a torrent and it was a minute before he attempted to stem it.

"Une histoire vraiment tragique. Your father is an artist and be drinks himself to death. Your brother is an artist also and he does the same, and you are without money." He shook his head mournfully. "And now tell me, if you please, how was it that you happened to go this evening to the studio of Henri Larne?"

Travers managed to gather that she came into the club and was informed that as she was the only one available of the type required, she would have to take on another sitting. She admitted she was less annoyed than she had made out, for she needed the money.

"But why should you need the money?" Gallois asked gently. "M. Braque ceases then to supply you?"

Her cheeks flared, and the words were spat out with an intensity of fury.

"Lui! Un vieux salaud, un m—"

"Silence!" Gallois too was glaring. Then he shrugged his shoulders apologetically. *"Pardon, mais quand il est question des morts, on parle avec respect."*

"Dead!"

"Happily—or unhappily—yes. While you pose in that chair this afternoon at a quarter to six, he is being murdered."

She went limp. For a moment Travers wondered if she were going to faint. Then she roused herself.

"Moi, je n'en sais rien."

"But naturally you know nothing," he assured her. "And there is no reason why you should feel any pity. M. Braque arranges for you to leave the rue Vagnolles, and to establish you in this apartment. That is so, is it not? And where do you think that he obtains the money tor this superb apartment?"

In a flash that look of malevolence was on her face again.

"He told me he had a fortune in his hands. He said he would be enormously rich."

Gallois turned triumphantly to Travers. "At last, my friend, we arrive. And M. Braque, he tells you in what this fortune consists?"

But she knew no more. He had suddenly become generous with his money, and she had taken what he said for truth.

"And then came the disappointment," said Gallois, as if it had been his own. "He shows you that apartment and behold—it is only his own! Four rooms, which he is also to share, in the rue Jourdoise! He makes love economically, our good Braque. You tell him so. You spit on his new furniture and you remain in the rue Vagnolles till he finds the flat which he promises."

Her frightened eyes were never off his face, but his own were across the room as if he were talking to himself.

"It is not for me to arrange the affairs of others, but it desolates me to think that one like yourself should be prepared to domesticate herself with this Braque. It is strange even that you should associate with such a one at all."

It had been his arranging, she said. It was only six months since she met him in a restaurant where she was dining with a mutual friend. As he was a picture dealer and she was hard-up, she showed him one of her brother's pictures—the only one she had—and he promised to sell it. Then later he proposed other arrangements instead.

Gallois was shaking his head as he got to his feet.

"I understand. All the same, you had a grievance against him because of the flat. One less understanding than myself might have had suspicions that were serious. But I know that when he was murdered, you were in the studio of M. Larne."

"But M. Larne, he also knows that I was not here."

"Exactly." He made a gesture of finality, then moved towards the door. "Now if you will be so good as to go downstairs, you shall be taken to the rue Vagnolles. To-morrow, perhaps, there are other things which I shall ask."

There was still a look of fright on her face as she got to her feet. Gallois showed her to the top of the landing, then came quickly back.

"She is not without good looks—that one. But to the window, my friend," he said. "There is, as I tell you, a comedy which is about to play itself."

CHAPTER VI
GALLOIS CONCLUDES

GALLOIS HAD SWITCHED OFF the light and now he whisked back the curtain and gently raised the window. Before Travers could look out, there were curious sounds from the pavement below. An angry voice was demanding something. Another voice was joining in, and a third. Then Travers could see a sort of confused movement of men in the shadow beyond the light from the shop window and there was the shriek of a woman's voice, and then the struggling group seemed to dissolve. A man was running and others after him. He was lost in the shadows again, then reappeared in the brief light of a distant street-lamp, and it seemed that he was outdistancing his pursuers. Nearer was the sound of a moving car.

"Descendons!" said Gallois, making for the door.

Travers emerged to find the pavement deserted. Gallois made for the gendarme who was still on guard at the shop door.

What is it? What happens?

Travers gathered that some pig had insulted the police and had ended by striking a certain Maximilien.

"And the woman? Where is she?"

She had just left in the car, the man said, and he had understood that it was by the Inspector's own orders.

"Everything disarranges itself," Gallois said exasperatedly. It seemed to Travers that he was about to speak more of his mind, but a car was drawing up. It was the police ambulance, and more men must have been about, for almost at once the body was brought down, and the doctor departed with it.

"All this is part of your comedy?" Travers asked dryly.

Gallois parted his arm. "Have patience, my friend, and you also will find it a comedy. Now we mount again and decide what it is best to do."

The light had been left on in the living-room and he closed the window and drew the curtain. Almost at once there was a sound in the kitchen, then in the passage, and Charles was entering the room. He was breathing hard but his quick glance at Travers was one of friendly impudence.

"Everything went well?" demanded Gallois in French.

"Superbly," said Charles impassively.

"She observed you well?"

"At close quarters," Charles told him with the same impassiveness.

Gallois smiled sadly. "Why so gloomy, then? At your age I was never given a job half so romantic."

A quick flicker of amusement passed across Charles's face.

"And Cointeau?" Gallois said.

"That is arranged."

"Then we go," Gallois said. "And you go too. It will still be necessary, of course, for you to dissociate yourself from the police."

Another quick flicker of amusement, and Charles was going. Gallois watched him as he went through the door. Travers was watching him too, for he had suddenly noticed a something which had vaguely interested him before. That brief smile on the face of Charles had given some singular resemblance to Gallois himself.

"You interest yourself also in that young man?"

Travers started, then smiled.

"What an uncanny aptitude you have for reading people's thoughts."

"But no," Gallois told him modestly. "All the same, one interests one's self in a pupil, and of this Charles I have hopes. Science marches, my friend, and it is the young who march with it. One day this little Charles becomes a someone. When I retire and devote myself to literature and art, there is someone who fills my shoes, as you say." He shrugged his shoulders resignedly. "Meanwhile he remains the pupil."

"And the player of comedies."

"Precisely. You understand the plot of this comedy that we play?"

"Yes," said Travers, "though I don't know that I'd quite call it a comedy. I take it your men pretended to handle that model roughly. Charles was coming opportunely by and protested. There was a squabble and he knocked a man down, and bolted. To-morrow he'll recognize her somewhere, and re-introduce himself. The rest—well, there we are."

Gallois caught the irony of his tone.

"It is not with me myself that you are displeased?"

Travers smiled. "But I'm not displeased."

"My friend, you deceive yourself," Gallois told him sadly. "I study, as you know, the methods of your Scotland Yard, which are the most admirable in the world. But they are for the English criminals. Here one is different. One adapts one's self to the methods of one's own assassins. At the moment I am not Lautin Gallois. I am the fighter of assassins. But it is with the brain that I fight. If necessary I use other weapons also, but for the moment I am the artist. Everything depends on *messieurs les assassins.*"

"You're right," Travers said, and was glancing at the clock.

"Before ten o'clock you will be back at your hotel," Gallois told him. "You would like to accompany me to the shop of M. Cointeau where we break the desolate news?"

"Most decidedly," Travers said. "And don't worry about me. I'm prepared to stay up all night."

Gallois took his arm affectionately.

"My friend, do not speak as if it is I who confer the favours. Without you I arrive nowhere. This is an affair of the two of us. You observe everything with myself, and you employ the methods that are your own. Every facility that you need, it is yours."

Then a look of consternation was coming over his face.

"But I forget. You pass a holiday here. You have affairs of your own."

"My idea of a holiday is to find out the truth about Braque."

"But madame your wife?" Gallois asked roguishly, and now it was in his face that Travers could see a queer resemblance to Charles. Then he smiled too.

"I expect that that also could arrange itself."

"Telephone, then, at once to madame," Gallois said, "and assure her that by ten o'clock you will have returned. I also have things to do, and then you and I will visit the shop of the admirable Cointeau."

The Boulevard Bastide is inconspicuous enough, and the shop of the partners, Cointeau and Braque, was even more so, for it was the short side of its rectangle that faced the boulevard, with the longer one running back into the rue Gévrance.

There was a side door at which Gallois knocked. A light was visible at once and soon Cointeau himself was opening the door. He was a man of over sixty, short and inclined to stoutness.

Gallois introduced himself and said he had bad news to report about Braque. There had been an accident.

"Entrez, messieurs," Cointeau said calmly, and his hand went out to the switch that lighted the shop.

"You allow us to go up?" Gallois said. "We shall be more at our ease upstairs and we don't wish to announce everything to all the world."

The upstair room was a living-room that seemed to have admitted work much as the Arab of the fable admitted the camel. Pictures and frames were everywhere, and on the table was an unframed picture that Cointeau had evidently been cleaning. A smell of methylated spirits was in the air. Cointeau seemed a phlegmatic soul who had known sufficient of the kicks of fortune to be able to accept with equanimity any new disaster, but he was certainly startled enough at what Gallois had to tell.

"You yourself were here at a quarter to six?" Gallois asked suggestively.

Cointeau thought hard, then said he was in the shop. There had been a possible client with whom he had been talking business. He admitted he had never seen that client before and he did not know his name.

"You are married?"

"I am a widower these last six years," Cointeau said. "My evenings, as you observe, I generally occupy with work."

"And when did you last see your partner?"

"At nine o'clock this morning. He arrived here and at ten o'clock he said he had business. Since then I have not seen him. But, one moment. This afternoon he came in at about four o'clock. He said simply that he would see me later and then he went off again. Since then I've seen nothing of him."

"Do you know what his business was?"

Cointeau said he had no idea. Braque had been very secretive of late.

"Of late?" Gallois said, and gave a quick look ac Travers. "But we had better begin at the beginning. Tell us, if you please, how it was you first became associated with Georges Braque."

The history of the partnership was as follows. Cointeau had a small business in the rue des Vinaigriers, and ten years ago he became acquainted with Braque, who tried to sell him two of his own pictures. Out of that evolved the partnership. Braque put money into the concern which was moved to the Boulevard Bastide. Cointeau confessed he was a valuable partner. He made connections with the art schools, he knew infinitely more than his partner about painting, and it was he who began and managed a system whereby the firm's pictures were exhibited at hotels and high-class restaurants, which drew their own commission on sales.

"Then you've made money," said Gallois jocularly.

Cointreau said he didn't know about that, but they had managed to buy the property, and they had survived the slump. Then about a year ago, Braque began to change. He said he had a scheme which he did not confide, whereby big money might be made, It took him away for periods varying from a day or two to a week, and then he confessed that what he had hoped was a gold-mine was after all not worth the candle.

"What he said first was 'risk,' and then when I demanded if it was something against the law, he excused himself. By 'risk' he said he meant risk of time and money, but I had the suspicion that he was involving himself with something else. That is why I was not surprised when you gentlemen came here to-night."

Cointeau had not the least idea what it was that Braque was even likely to be engaged in, unless it was a deal in pictures. Then about six months ago, he said, Braque had yet another scheme which he assured his partner was a veritable gold-mine. Again he did not divulge what the scheme was, but again there were the long absences.

"But this afternoon," said Cointeau, "something happened which I now prefer to relate. He came to the shop, as I told you, and announced that he would see me again later. I was annoyed and I said that all the work was on me, and we were losing business, and he was doing nothing. Then he felt in his pocket like this"—he made the motions of a man who hauls something from a hip-pocket—"and there is a bundle of notes, big as this. Thousands and thousands of francs there were, and then he laughed. 'The gold-mine already commences to produce dividends,' was what he said, and then he replaced the notes, and laughed again, and he was away and gone."

"Two gold-mines," said Gallois reflectively. "One was not worth, the risk, and the other commences already to produce dividends. But that gold-mine was also not worth the risk, if one is to he murdered and the dividends taken from one's pocket. But tell me, Monsieur Cointeau, as the man of standing and probity that you are. Did these travels of your partner ever lead him to Spain?"

Cointeau shrugged his broad shoulders and spread his pudgy hands in despair. He had no idea; no idea at all where his partner had spent his time.

"He took an interest in the great painters of, say, since the war?"

Cointeau explained regretfully that such things could scarcely interest the firm of Braque and Cointeau, who had not the available capital. They merely picked up the leavings of the big dealers, though more than once they had made lucky purchases and had unexpected windfalls.

"At the moment we have a sketch by Ingres, for which we ask forty thousand francs," he said. "That costs us five hundred francs, but that is a windfall that occurs rarely."

"You never had the good fortune to acquire a picture by Henri Larne?"

Cointeau smiled. "M'sicur l'Inspecteur amuses himself," he said.

"All the same, you never heard him mention the great Larne?"

Cointeau shrugged his shoulders. "But he mentions every painter. When one sells pictures, naturally one talks of painters."

"Naturally," said Gallois placatingly. "And that flat of his in the rue Jourdoise, what does he do there?"

"He sleeps there."

Gallois smiled bitterly. "Bur, of course, I didn't think of that." He got to his feet. "For to-night, that is all. To-morrow it will be necessary to examine any papers belonging to your late colleague."

"Here?"

"But certainly."

"I assure you there are no papers," Cointeau said earnestly. "There are the accounts of the business, and that is all. Why should he leave here any papers concerning his private affairs?"

"Then why should you make difficulties if the law considers it necessary to make certain?" Gallois challenged him. "If it is the upsetting of your business in the morning that you wish to avoid, I am at your service. The documents shall be examined at once. You will excuse me for a minute?"

He made a sign for Travers to remain. In a minute he was back and two men with him. Cointeau was ironically assured that everything would be done without fuss and with discretion.

"And now," Gallois said, when he and Travers came out to the pavement again, "it is still not ten o'clock. You are hungry?"

"I could eat a horse," Travers said.

Gallois turned back at once to the rue Gévrance.

"There is a restaurant that I know where one supplies everything. I also could devour a horse."

Almost at once he was stopping and entering an inconspicuous restaurant where he seemed to be well known. Within five minutes they were at a corner table by themselves and Gallois was serving the soup.

"You had your men ready to search the shop, then?" Travers said.

"Yes," Gallois said, "but it was necessary first to see the reactions of this Cointeau. You observe that he made objections to the search?"

"That was all in his favour," Travers said. "If he'd fallen in with your original suggestion that your men should arrive in the morning, then you might have assumed he was going to have a good look to-night for himself and remove anything incriminating."

"You also are a thought-reader," Gallois told him admiringly. "But about this Cointeau, I do not know. A man of his type, so naive, so candid, so patient with his colleague, does not probably exist."

"I rather liked him. It struck me that Braque was the flashy oily-tongued partner, always on the lookout for quick money. Cointeau was the honest drudge who kept things together."

"Nevertheless," Gallois said, "I should prefer to meet that client who will establish the alibi of our good Cointeau for a quarter to six to-night. That Cointeau confesses he saw the notes which the assassin took to-night from the pocket of Braque, that convinces me little. It is always best to admit what one knows will be discovered. It was natural also that Cointeau should admit that the firm suffers from the holidays of Braque, but what I think always is that Cointeau knows also the flat of Braque, and that there is a way by which one enters unperceived."

It was the quickest of meals they were eating, with a couple of soles to follow and *omelettes sucrées* to conclude. Gallois talked as quickly as he ate.

"Now, my friend," he said, "I explain to you things perhaps that you do not understand. When you come to me with your story of Braque, I receive what one calls a shock. There is a certain matter which already brings him to our notice, but we possess no evidence and we do nothing. All the same, we observe and we enquire." He shrugged his shoulders. "But there appears nothing wrong with the admirable Braque, and we disregard, and it is at that moment, my friend, that you arrive."

"What did you suspect him of?" asked Travers quickly.

"That he smuggles pictures," Gallois said. "This affair so terrible in Spain, it lends itself to thieving, does it not? One destroys a town, but is it sure that one destroys also the *objets d'art?* In the churches there are pictures of enormous value. There are the private collections which are also pillaged. We receive applications from the authorities, and this man Braque, who pays a visit to Spain, is under suspicion. But, as I tell you, we discover nothing."

Travers had taken off his glasses and now he was slowly polishing them.

"I'm beginning to see things. Braque came to England to get into contact with private collectors. He summed up their characters, and, when he thought it would be safe, he gave a hint that he had things they might like to see. What he'd have shown me to-night was some stolen masterpiece, but the murderer was aware that he was bringing it to the flat, and he killed him and got away with the picture."

"And the money?"

"The murderer naturally went through his pockets to remove anything incriminating," Travers said.

"And that interest in the pictures of Henri Larne?"

"There," said Travers dryly, "I am also of the opinion of yourself. One of the pictures which Braque acquired from Spain was a Larne. It puzzled him to place its value. Hence the enquiries in England. In England, in fact, Braque was killing two birds with one stone."

"That is superb," Gallois said, and reached across the table to give his hand a complimentary pat. "Braque sells to some client who prefers to ask no questions. He vaunts his money to Cointeau this afternoon. He also has spent money—but not too much—on the woman Deschamps, whose real name, I should also inform you, is Elise Moulins. All that is simple, but there is a difficulty which remains. There were, if you remember, two goldmines, It is the second gold-mine with which we occupy ourselves. What, then, was the first?"

"There you have me beaten," Travers said. "It was doubtless some swindle or other. But, need we worry ourselves about it? Would it be more profitable to stick to what we know? To try to discover what pictures Braque did get from Spain, for instance?"

"But the pictures are sold," Gallois reminded him. "It was thousands and thousands of francs that he flourished before the eyes of the simple Cointeau."

"There remains the picture which the murderer took," Travers said. "The picture which I should have seen, and didn't."

"There, perhaps, it will be you who make the enquiries," Gallois said. "M. Larne will give us a record of all the pictures which pass from his possession, and one can also enquire from the dealers. To-morrow, at breakfast, you will receive papers of authorization and identity. The whole of Paris is at your disposal, as it is at mine."

He was waving impatiently for his omelette to be brought, and then at once he went on.

"What you should also know is this. This evening I take precautions, as you know. One keeps you under observation from the time you arrive at the rue Jourdoise. At a quarter to six one had under observation the flat of Braque, and five minutes later I arrive. There is a light beneath the door and we know then that Braque is already there." Once more he shrugged his shoulders. "No one enters and no one leaves, which is simple. Braque was dead and his assassin had disappeared before we surround the flat."

"But that wasn't your fault."

"It was what one calls the bad luck," Gallois said, and spread his hands resignedly. "We anticipate no danger to yourself. We surround the flat so that there is no means of removing the stolen picture which he shows you."

He drank the last of his wine and was waiting for Travers to finish his hasty meal.

"And what for to-morrow?" Travers said.

"In the morning you shall be informed. This affair intrigues you?"

"More than a case ever did before."

"And myself also," Gallois said. "It is a case that is worthy of our attention. Not an affair of routine where one wastes one's talent." He got to his feet. "Now I drive you to your hotel, and then I return to the rue Jourdoise."

Outside the hotel be shook Travers warmly by the hand, and smiled with a melancholy approval.

"The disagreeable I shall perform for myself," he said. "To-morrow it is possible that Cointeau and the woman Deschamps will be asked to identify the dead Braque."

"Why didn't you take her in to see him at the flat?"

"There one is too much at one's ease," Gallois remarked sadly. "It is at the Morgue that one studies best the reactions."

A wave of the hand and he was off. Travers was still wincing at the thought of the Morgue, and as he stood there in the cold drizzle, he felt a quick depression that was remarkably akin to fear. Suavity and finesse there might be in the methods of Gallois, but there was also a ruthlessness and a grim directness of purpose that were terrifying; and as a car drew up across the road with a squeak of its brakes, he thought of the darkness of the rue Jourdoise, and the shriek of the woman Deschamps, and the hand clapped over her mouth.

CHAPTER VII
TRAVERS HAS IDEAS

BERNICE WOULD HAVE been alarmed if her husband had not so dexterously cast a kind of matter-of-factness over that affair in the rue Jourdoise. He had happened to discover a body and that was all. Braque had turned out to be some kind of rascal, and it was only the particular kind of rascal that the police, with the naturally necessary help of himself, were wanting to find out.

Bernice pretended a grievance.

"So I'm to be a widow once more."

"That was a golfing widow," he told her. "This is a—well, a widowhood of convenience. Two or three days and it should be all over. As it is, I can't get out of it."

"Poor darling," she said. "All the same, I expect you're enjoying it already; you and M. Gallois." She sighed. "While you're enjoying yourself this morning, I'm having my hair done, and that's always so trying."

She caught his look, and they laughed.

"Ah, well," said Travers. "If absences make hearts fonder, then widowhood ought to cement them for life."

She was away and gone soon after nine o'clock, and then who should appear but Charles, bringing the papers that Gallois had mentioned. There was also a note to the effect that Gallois hoped to call not later than ten o'clock.

"You do speak some English?" Travers asked Charles.

Charles smiled apologetically. He spoke very little indeed, he said, but he was studying hard. It was M. Gallois' idea that he should equip himself with a perfect English. M. Gallois had always taken an interest in his career. But if Mr. Travers could put up with his imperfect English, he would try it.

"You're a fortunate young fellow," Travers said. "By the way, Charles, how old are you?"

"Twenty-four, monsieur."

"You look younger," Travers said. "It is permitted that you and I talk about the case?"

"But certainly," Charles said. "You are a collaborator."

His snub nose lent a roguishness to his smile, and he certainly seemed much more relaxed now he was out of the company of his Inspector.

"Then wasn't there an affair of gallantry on your hands this morning?"

"Ah, that," he said, and grinned. "That is already over. This morning I happened to be near the rue Vagnolles, and it is she who recognizes me. As I am still afraid of the *flics,* we go inside a restaurant and take coffee. This evening we go to a cinema."

"You've learnt anything?"

Charles shook his head. "In these affairs it is necessary that one moves slowly. But she is a type that is sympathetic and I have hopes."

"Hopes to learn, what?"

"Who knows? Who are the associates of Braque, perhaps. Something he lets fall about this fortune that he is about to make."

"Exactly. And you recognize in this affair also a danger for yourself?"

"A danger?"

Travers smiled. "When one wins the confidence of someone who is also sympathetic, there is the danger that one may fall in love."

"Ne vous inquietez pas, monsieur," Charles told him confidently. "She is not a type so sympathetic as that."

Gallois accepted Travers's offer of coffee in a corner of the deserted lounge. He had snatched an hour or two's sleep he said and had eaten early. Travers told him how he had attempted to pull the leg of his protégé Charles.

"Love," said Gallois with a smile of dismissal. "One learns not to mix that with one's serious affairs."

"But what about your own young days?"

For a moment the eyes of Gallois lifted reflectively to the ceiling.

"Youth has its frivolities," he said, "but for my part I had neither the money nor the leisure. When one adopts my profession, one ceases at once to be young. The blood dries in the veins, which is why I direct myself in my—hobbies, is it not that you call them?—to the intellectual and not the frivolous. That is also perhaps why I achieve a certain success. But about this affair with which we occupy ourselves. You have perhaps some ideas?"

"One thing only I've been thinking," Travers said. "Braque was killed at the front door, though the murderer doubtless escaped by the back."

"You mean, because his body lay at that front door?"

"Yes," said Travers. "Therefore Braque admitted the murderer at the front door and was at once stabbed. One gathers that, because the murderer had to work quickly. But the idea that came to me was this. Did Braque overstep himself? Did he think he had found someone—like myself, for instance—who would be likely to buy a fine picture and ask no questions, but was that somebody as big a rascal as himself?"

Gallois made a note in his book. "What you think is this. Braque have two strings to his bow. He arranges to see this rascal, this assassin, before he arranges to see you. If he sell the picture before he sees you, then to you he will be most apologetic. If he do not, then there is, as you say, no harm done." He nodded to himself. "That is an idea which is worthy of consideration. But first I ask a question which surprises you, my friend." He leaned forward, coffee cup balanced precariously. *"Was it Braque that arranged the visit with you?"*

Travers stared, then his fingers were at his glasses.

"I wonder," he said. "I took it for granted it was Braque. But, now I remember, there was something different, and the phone was very bad." Then he, too, was leaning forward. "If it was not Braque who rang me, who was it?"

"It was *not* Braque," Gallois told him confidently. "Braque did not prepare as he would have prepared for you. He did not shave, and his hands were dirty and his linen was not clean. It was the assassin who rang you in the name of Braque, and arranged that you should go to the rue Jourdoise at six o'clock. Then in your name he doubtless rang Braque and said that you would arrive at—shall we say?—half-past five. Perhaps he was unable to find Braque till it was almost the time, and therefore Braque have not the time to shave. He opens the door to admit you and he prepares to make the apologies, but it is the assassin that he admits. Before he can exclaim, he is dead."

"Then this assassin is someone who knew my affairs very intimately," Travers said. "That's a very disturbing thought."

Gallois smiled patiently. "For us it is not disturbing. The assassin plays, as you say, into our hands. *Tiens, mon ami.*"

He tore a page from his notebook.

"Let us write the things at which we arrive. This assassin, what does he know? That Braque speaks English very badly, and therefore, as he cannot imitate the bad English of Braque, he requests that he speak to you in French. This assassin knows also that you have dealings with Braque who wishes that you should come to his apartment, and he knows also your address in Paris. What then remains to do? Only, my friend, that we write down all those to whom you impart such things—and, you will pardon?—to whom madame, your wife, perhaps, impart such things, and whose English is so bad that he cannot even speak it badly. Then without doubt we write the name of the assassin."

But Travers was all at once frowning away, and his fingers went to his glasses.

"You discover something?" Gallois asked anxiously.

"I don't know," Travers said slowly. "But there's someone who seems to me to fulfil most of the conditions. Pierre Larne!"

"Ah!" said Gallois, and his eyes suddenly narrowed. "He is the attendant of his famous brother, but what you call in England, hanger-on. His brother tells him about yourself. What is it that you know yourself already about this Pierre?"

Travers told him everything he knew, and gave his own impressions.

"Now I also tell something," Gallois said. "Already you have mentioned to me this Pierre, and it is necessary that I make enquiries. This Pierre Larne, the half-brother, he is one who spends much money. He is a parasite, and I explain. Henri Larne is not the type that has need of a secretary. He is not what one calls fashionable, with a salon, and domestics and everything that is necessary. He is simply a painter and he is also a Bohemian. He paints also, as I already say, only when he feels a spiritual force. I do not express myself very well, but you understand. For his pictures he receives sums that are considerable, but when one paints little and one is a genius, there is no need that one should employ a secretary or an agent to manage the affairs. Also he himself spends the money that he gains. You commence, my friend, to have ideas?"

"I think perhaps I do," Travers told him. "Pierre is a parasite and Henri is too good-natured to shake him off. But two people can't burn the same candle, and at both its ends. Suppose, then, that Henri has had to call a halt; to tell Pierre that he can't support him any longer, then Pierre might have tried making easy money in other ways. In association with Braque, for instance."

"My friend, you have a perception that is miraculous. This Pierre perhaps conceives the idea of selling the pictures of his brother. It is Braque who sells and one divides what one makes."

He caught sight of his coffee, grimaced as he tasted its coldness, then set down the empty cup.

"You will pardon me? It is necessary to change the arrangements, and that I should telephone."

It was a quarter of an hour before he came back and he seemed very pleased with himself.

"I speak to M. Larne," he said, "and I say that you arrive with news which you will explain. It is necessary also to see the brother. That also he arranges."

"But what am I to do?"

"In half an hour you arrive," Gallois told him, "so we have the time to make our preparations. But what I suggest myself is this . . ."

It was a woman who opened the door: a gaunt, hard-featured woman of fifty who was evidently cleaning up the lower rooms. Almost before Travers could say a word, Henri Larne was coming quickly down the stairs.

"Merci, Hortense," he said, and motioned for her to go.

"I'm not disturbing you?" Travers said.

"Not at all," Larne said. "The work is finished. I began again at five o'clock this morning. The American collector should arrive here at noon."

Travers glanced at his watch.

"I oughtn't to keep you for more than a few minutes. I think you'll be very interested, by the way. Your brother's here?"

"Upstairs," he said. "Come along and let's hear all this important news."

Pierre was looking out of the studio window, and what struck Travers about him that morning was not that he was ill at ease but that he was trying not to appear so. He held out his hand to Travers, and it was somewhat awkwardly that he took the seat which Henri indicated.

"My news is about Braque," Travers began.

"Braque? You have discovered something?"

Travers began to tell him about the smuggling theory. Pierre was listening with such a strained intentness, that Travers realized he was being left somewhat out.

"Will you put up with my French? Your brother might be interested."

"But you speak an admirable French," Henri said. "One makes one's self understood, and there is nothing else needed."

So Travers began again and went on with his story in French. Even before he had finished, Henri was shaking his head.

"I'm afraid we can't help. Neither of us has any recollection of any dealings with a Spanish client. You understand, of course, that we shouldn't be aware of the fact if a picture had been re-sold privately."

"Then there's no use asking you for records," Travers said. He smiled as he got to his feet. "That was really all I came for, so I'll leave you to prepare for your American."

"No, no," Henri said hurriedly. "There were other things I wanted you to hear." He clicked his tongue exasperatedly. "Ever since that affair last night I haven't been able to think clearly. You wouldn't believe what a shock it was to me to discover that I knew Braque. Ah!"—his face lighted up—"now I know what it was that I wanted to tell you. Isn't there a perfectly good reason why he should be interested in my pictures?"

"I quite agree," Travers said. "Naturally he'd he interested in you as an old contemporary at the Académie Poussin." He smiled disarmingly again. "You understand, of course, that all these questions belong to M. Gallois. He did not wish to encroach on your privacy, so he sent me."

Henri smiled. "He is an exceedingly amiable character." The look became somewhat quizzical. "It was a surprise, however, to find you in the company of the police."

Travers explained. He said also that he was hedged in with confidences.

"M. Gallois knows nothing, for instance, of those strange happenings you told me about. The attempted burglary and so on."

"My friend, I hope you would never dream that I should suspect you of betraying a confidence," Larne said. "You are a man of honour, and you are my friend, but now you mention that attempted burglary, or whatever it was, there's something else you should hear. At half-past five last night—"

"It was later than that," broke in Pierre.

Henri turned almost angrily on him.

"That clock there"—it was the clock on the studio mantelpiece that he was indicating—"was under my eye. I tell you I had just begun to work when you drove the car in."

"Listen one moment," Pierre said patiently.

"First there is something I do to the car, then I come to the door and it is locked and I remember that I cannot give you the message as you are to be undisturbed. Then I go to the car again, and then I think that I will leave the message with Hortense, since I do not return. It is while I speak with Hortense that I hear this noise and I investigate. Hortense hears it too, and when I call out, 'Who is there?' she hears the men running."

"It was dark. How did you know they were men?"

"I hear one speak to another, then they disappeared through the hedge."

Henri's lip drooped. "And naturally you did not follow. The mouse does not suddenly become a lion. And what was it that Hortense heard?"

Pierre shrugged his shoulders as if the affair, as far as he was concerned, was over.

"You permit?" said Henri exasperatedly, and called to Hortense from the door.

She looked distinctly disquieted. Henri repeated to her what Pierre had said, and there was almost a contempt in his tone as if Pierre were unreliable and she was well aware of it. But she bore out the story. She had heard men's voices and had heard the crashing through the hedge.

"And what time was this?" asked Henri, with scarcely veiled incredulity.

"I had given Bertrand his medicine," she said, "so it was after half-past five. It was about a quarter to six. There is something also that I wish to say."

"Well?"

She spoke more and more rapidly, and soon Travers was understanding nothing, but from the gesticulations and a chance word or two he gathered that these affairs were frightening her, and she was refusing to stay. Henri joined in, hands quivering with anger, and when Pierre put in a word, he was contemptuously silenced.

Then the storm ceased as suddenly as it had begun. Hortense departed with thanks for something that Travers had not gathered. Pierre rose too and said he would he going. Travers rose also, and once more Henri insisted that he should remain.

"Things become wearisome here," he said to Travers when they were alone.

There followed an explanation about Hortense. She and her husband occupied the kind of chalet beyond the trees at the extreme end of the villa garden. She was general domestic of the villa, and her husband, who had been badly gassed in the war, pottered about in the gardens. Now he was tubercular, and in a serious way.

"Do not repeat these apparent generosities of mine," Larne said to Travers, "If people attach these bourgeois virtues to my name, before long everyone will say that after all I am a bourgeois, which will be the end of me. But to-morrow I am sending Bertrand to a place where he may have more care, and everything here will be shut up. Where I shall go I do not know. Perhaps I shall remain in Paris."

"I'm sorry about it all," Travers said. "I don't think the police will trouble you any more."

"I don't mind the police." He gave another gesture of weariness. "It is these other things that disturb my work." A shake or two of the head and his lip was drooping ironically again. "You also suffer from relations?"

"God forbid," said Travers. "But I know what some kinds can be."

"I have this Pierre—"

Then he broke off. "But I will not bore you with my private affairs. Besides, I have come to the end. After to-day there will be a different arrangement. That is why I ask you should still not mention to a soul this curious affair of last night."

His eyes narrowed and he was looking thoughtfully across the room, then he turned to Travers as if he had made up his mind about something.

"In confidence, my friend, you believe this story that you have just heard?"

"But why not?" asked Travers, surprised. "The woman heard things as well. Undoubtedly it was the men who broke in here before. There was no light and they thought the place was shut up."

"Yes, and suppose that no thieves broke in here at all last time. Suppose that was a—a fake. Suppose these noises last night were also a fake, to give a reality to the first affair, of which, perhaps, I have shown signs of doubt."

Travers raised his eyebrows. "But there was no fake about that attempt on your life?"

"You are right," he said slowly. "That was no fake. But I beg of you forget all about this. I had no right to trouble you with my affairs."

He walked with Travers to the gate.

"Good luck to the picture," Travers said. "I wish I'd been able to see it again."

"At the moment I am a Philistine," Larne told him, with something of his old careless good-humour. "The picture has ceased to interest me. The important thing now is the cheque."

Travers looked back along the road, and Larne was still at the gate to give him a last wave of the hand—a gesture so English and so friendly, that Travers felt a tremendous sympathy. And he was also profoundly puzzled, and it was Pierre who was the enigma. In his mind's eye he could still see him, weak-chinned and with well-fed face, sitting there and taking without protest the sneers of his half-brother, uttered though they were in the presence of a guest, and the woman Hortense.

And then Travers began to see daylight. Gallois had been accurate in his description of Pierre Larne. He was a parasite and Henri had grown tired. He had warned him that he was at the end of his tether, and when the cheque of the American was received, then Pierre would receive a final paying-off.

But Pierre had seen that danger approaching, and he had already turned in other directions for money. He had faked a burglary, and this business of last night was, as Henri Larne had revealed, merely another fake to bolster up the first. It would have been easy enough to convince Hortense—hard-bitten though she looked—that there were voices, and, as for the crashing through the hedge, that could have been done by Pierre himself.

Henri Larne had also lied, but to shield his half-brother. When he said that nothing had been taken, he was hiding the truth. What had been taken was one or some of those sketches and studies. Anything by the great Larne was of value, and collectors would be glad to buy it. *And the selling agent for these purloined pictures had been Braque,* and it was a study by Henri Larne that he himself would have been shown by Braque at the flat in the rue Jourdoise.

That those deductions were correct, Travers had no vestige of doubt. One difficulty remained. Who was it that had murdered Braque? Then even about that Travers began to have ideas. There must have been a third party to the thefts, and it was this third party who had double-crossed both his confederates, and who now knew that Pierre would be too terrified to talk.

But Travers's report to Gallois was necessarily guarded, for there were the confidences of Henri Larne to respect. He did, however, mention the cleavage between the brothers, and the probability that Pierre had already been kept short of money.

"You think of him as a likely confederate of Braque," Gallois said with a directness that Travers once more found disconcerting.

"The mere fact that he was who he was, would bring him into contact with dealers," hedged Travers. "But it wasn't he who did the killing. He has an alibi which two witnesses can back up. Henri Larne himself, and the woman domestic at the villa, can prove he was there at about a quarter to six."

"This Pierre is not the type that murders," Gallois said. "But about this afternoon, my friend. I have business which is official. I explain the conduct of this affair to my superiors, but meanwhile the affair must not rest. You would wish to see the good Cointeau, perhaps, who might reveal to you things he would not reveal to us."

"I think I would like to see Cointeau," Travers said. "What I'd rather do first is to go to that flat in broad daylight, to see things and fix them in my mind."

Gallois smiled. "And when you go to the rue Jourdoise, you also go with ideas?"

Travers shook his head amusedly.

"You're an uncanny sort of bird, you know, Gallois. Perhaps I have got ideas. All the same, I'm not telling them to you till I see how they work out."

CHAPTER VIII
DISCOVERIES

THE FRONT DOOR of the flat was sealed, and the door of the empty shop as well. Travers took a first view of the back where there was a tiny yard which led direct into the rue Robertin. A gendarme was on duty at the foot of the short stairway that led to the flat, and Travers found the door open.

"*Qui est là?*"

There were steps in the passage, and in came Charles.

"*Ah, monsieur, c'est vous.*"

"What are you doing here?" Travers asked. "I thought you had temporarily broken off relationships with the police."

Charles grinned. "One uses care, that is all."

"And what are you actually doing here?"

There had been no finger-prints, no incriminating papers—nothing, he said. He was now searching the flat in case by chance something of value might have been overlooked. Travers mentioned his own wish to see everything by daylight, and said that he and Charles would not disturb each other.

"But I have finished," Charles said. "If you wish me, I am at your service."

Travers inspected the flat with Charles at his elbow. In each room he cast a look at the ceiling. When they reached the living-room, Charles said gently that there was no communication with the attic that belonged to the former junk-shop.

"You also are a reader of thoughts," Travers told him amusedly. "What other ideas do you think I've got?"

"You permit?" said Charles. "In the room from which one has now removed the new furniture, you look out of the window and you nod appreciatively to yourself. You say to yourself, perhaps, that Elise is right to be indignant at the offer of a flat with so bad a view."

"Right first time," Travers told him cheerfully.

"It is nothing," Charles told him. "One is taught to observe, but there is a pleasure in observing monsieur."

"And what have you observed in this particular room?"

Charles shrugged his shoulders as much as to say that if Travers wanted to hear the obvious, he could be told it.

"You look at the floor, monsieur, and that mark on the boards, and one gathers that you do not like too much the sight of blood. Then you look round the room and it is the pictures that interest you, as they did last night."

"Yes," Travers said, "and in this light they look more atrocious than ever. Shall we take that one down?"

It was the landscape he meant, which was about three feet by two. Together they lifted it off its hook and laid it face down on the table. In a moment Travers was opening a blade of his penknife.

"You are going to cut the picture from the frame?" Charles said.

Travers wrestled with technicalities in French. One did not cover the back of an oil-painting with paper, as one covered a water-colour. And in spite of its dust, this paper looked curiously new.

"There is something beneath the paper?" asked Charles, eyes agog.

"We'll see," said Travers, and was ripping it off.

Beneath was a thin backing of wood, which was most certainly new, and the small iron sprigs that held it were new and scarcely rusted. Travers snapped the blade of his knife in his impatience at getting them out, and Charles was also wrenching them loose with his fingers. Then at last that backing came out and beneath it was a canvas, fixed to a thin wooden frame.

"It is this that you seek?" Charles said, eyes still agog.

"Yes," said Travers, "and shall I tell you what I think it is. It is a picture that is modern, and in the corner will be a small donkey that flies."

He hoisted the frame and shook that hidden canvas out. Charles grabbed it as it fell, and was taking the first look.

"Monsieur, there is no donkey."

The face of Travers was comical in its dismay. What he was looking at was no study by Henri Larne. Nor was it some study in pornography. It was a picture of a bull-fight, and nine-teenth-century at that.

Then he smiled, even if it was ruefully, and his hand fell on Charles's shoulder.

"We've shot the wrong bird."

"But it is a bird?"

"Oh, yes," said Travers. "It's a bird, and a valuable bird."

He took it nearer the window, polished his glasses and had a good look at it. Then suddenly he thought of something.

"When this house was searched, was there by any chance a pair of pincers?"

Charles stared, then looked annoyed.

"What a fool I am! There were pincers in his bedroom."

"You see the point?" Travers said when Charles came back with them. "Kept in his bedroom, in a drawer. If I, or someone, came to whom he thought he dared exhibit, this hidden picture, the pincers would be handy. Out would come the sprigs in no time, and, if necessary, back they would go again."

"And this picture, monsieur, what is it?"

"A Goya. Francisco Goya."

Charles looked blank, then his face brightened.

"There may be a picture behind that other also."

"Just what I was thinking," Travers told him. "Which is one reason why I asked about the pincers."

The second picture was much smaller, and behind it was a panel: the bust of an ecclesiastic in his robes.

"Spanish, and seventeenth-century," Travers said. "I'd almost be inclined to say Velasquez, but I didn't know that he painted anything as small."

"These are the pictures that were smuggled from Spain?"

"It certainly looks like it," Travers said. "They've probably been hidden here for some time while Braque looked round for possible clients. What he did was to look out for two pictures—and the more rubbishy, the better—which would exactly fit; then he covered the backs with paper and threw plenty of dust on." He was suddenly looking up. "I wonder. Would these be the only pictures, do you think? The wallpaper's discoloured—look!—where these two were. What about trying to find if there's a discoloration anywhere else?"

But there was never a trace. Charles asked why Travers was shaking his head.

"Things don't quite fit in," Travers said. "If there was no other picture, then what did the murderer come here to get? Also, if Braque expected a possible customer for a picture, why hadn't he the picture out of its hiding-place and ready?"

"He was waiting until he had made sure of that customer," suggested Charles. "The customer who was to come before you yourself arrived. The customer who happened also to be the assassin."

"I expect you're right," Travers told him. "Will you arrange for a taxi while I telephone?"

He rang up the only picture dealers he knew in Paris—the Schiffler Brothers—and asked for Joseph Schiffler. Joseph was out but expected back by the rime Travers would arrive. Then Travers remembered something else.

"There is no necessity that you should remain here?" he asked Charles. "If not, may I advise something? That you go to Cointeau's shop and examine *every* picture. If there is one oil-painting whose back is covered, then make your examination. In half an hour I hope to be there too."

Then he stopped at the door.

"First it would be wise, would it not, to remove carefully these two atrocities, and the paper and the little nails. See M. Gallois, if it is possible, and report that there has been a discovery. There is also an expert, perhaps, who will be able to say how long it is since Braque concealed these pictures which I now take with me for examination." He picked up one of the sprigs. "There is rust that can be seen, perhaps, under a microscope, and your people will be able to make certain tests."

Charles nodded. All that, he said, would be immediately arranged.

The Boulevard San Michel crosses the Seine, and it was at the southern end that was situated the establishment of the Schifflers. It was an unpretentious place, yet through the hands of the Schifflers there probably passed more pictures of supreme quality than were handled by the rest of the big dealers combined.

Joseph Schiffler, looking more like a rabbi than ever, was delighted to see Travers, even if he did cast more than one private glance at the pictures which an attendant brought in at Travers's heels.

Travers told him in confidence the whole story.

"Ah, the *affaire* Braque!" he said. "One reads of it already in the papers, but not as related by you, my friend. You permit that I see these pictures?"

Travers showed him the bull-fight. He gave a little grunt at the sight of it, and then took it to the window. His old eyes peered closely, and then from his pocket he produced a glass.

"In your opinion it is a Goya?"

"Unmistakably so."

The old man smiled dryly. "In this life there is always the possibility of mistakes. But there is something which will interest you."

It was not the picture he meant, but something in the book whose pages be was now turning—Antoine Rabeau's life of Goya.

"There is your picture," he said, and there indeed was a photograph of the Goya that Braque had hidden. From the text Travers saw that the picture was a late work, "now in the collection of the Marquis Hautgarde."

"There is the explanation that you seek," Schiffler said. "The Marquis is French, and for some years has occupied his villa at Malaga. And this war in Spain, it reached Malaga, did it not?"

The other picture intrigued the old man still more. It was a Zurbaran, he said, and Travers was glad he had given no opinions of his own. It had been tampered with, he said, and would Travers permit calling in another member of the firm, whose opinion should be valuable.

Travers added more explanations, He had an urgent appointment, he said, and the whole thing could be left to the discretion and at the convenience of the firm.

"Within two hours you shall know as much as we," Schiffler said. "Your address is?"

Travers requested that the information should be sent direct to Gallois at the Sûreté, but he himself would take the firm's receipt.

"You had naturally never heard of this Braque till you read of the *affaire*?" Travers asked him while he was writing.

The old man shook his head. But he would make discreet enquiries, he said, and that information should also be passed direct to M. Gallois.

Travers had a preliminary glance through the glazed door of Cointeau's shop, and there was Charles at work, and an anxious-looking Cointeau accompanying him. Cointeau stared at the sight of Travers.

Travers explained that he had come in order to see that M. Cointeau was disturbed as little as possible.

"If anyone enters," he said, "I am at once a client, but a client who can wait. As for this gentleman here, who examines the pictures, he can be explained as a new assistant."

Charles took advantage of the opportunity to have a rest. It was fatiguing work, he said, hoisting off pictures and hoisting them back again. He had seen M. Gallois and given an account of the extra-ordinary discovery.

"He was surprised?" Travers asked.

Charles shrugged his shoulders. "It is impossible to tell. He wears a mask, that one."

"And our friend there?" Travers nodded in the direction of the watchful Cointeau. "He knows what you are looking for?"

Charles said he had given him an idea and no more. It was Travers, then, who had a word with Cointeau while Charles resumed the examination of the oils. Cointeau was flabbergasted and it was with a cringing and apologetic haste that he dissociated himself from the doings of his late partner.

"But no one associates you," Travers assured him.

"You permit now that I assist in this examination?" Cointeau said energetically.

"In a minute," Travers said. "But about this partner of yours. You will miss him?"

Cointeau said he had already replaced him by a nephew of his own who at that very moment was out calling on the hotels and restaurants where the firm had pictures.

"He was a good business man, this Braque?"

Cointeau thought for a moment. Whatever the unlawful activities in which Braque had been engaged, he said, it was necessary to confess that he brought most of the business to the firm. There followed a quick reservation that such had been the case until the last year, when Braque had got into his head that idea of gold-mines.

"You haven't by any chance remembered anything else that he said to you about these goldmines?"

"Yes," said Cointeau. "This morning I remember something but it is something which does not make sense. Two or three days ago he comes here, and I am annoyed. I ask about this business and that, and he says 'All in good time'—like that. I say that this gold-mine looks like being the end of our affairs, and then I become angry. I become sarcastic. I say, where is it, this gold-mine? Perhaps he departs soon for America or South Africa, where there are real gold-mines. Then he laughs, and what he says is this. 'There is no reason why one should sail for America. There are gold-mines everywhere. To get to this gold-mine of my own, for instance, I take a taxi.'"

"And then?"

Cointeau's shrug of the shoulders was humiliation itself.

"And then, monsieur, he says no more. To me it was as if he knows he has said too much, and before I can speak, he waves his hand and off he goes."

"Take a taxi to a gold-mine," repeated Travers reflectively. "And what do you now think about that?"

Cointeau looked astonished. "But, monsieur, it is simple. It is to his flat that he takes the taxi, where he has hidden these pictures which have just been discovered. It is the pictures that are the goldmine." He gave himself a nod or two of approval.

"He was clever, was that one. He always did have the brains. I, I have the knowledge of affairs, but it is he who always had the ideas."

"Yes," said Travers, "and they ended with a knife in the ribs. And now I will look round your shop while you continue the examination of the pictures."

In a few minutes the electric light had to be switched on. The shop itself was finished with, and by the time the upstair rooms had been gone through, it was half-past five. Nothing whatever had been discovered. Charles approached Travers for a confidential word.

"Monsieur will allow me to depart? There is an appointment."

"Ah, yes." Travers smiled dryly as he remembered the meeting with Elise. "You regale yourself at the cinema."

"First we eat," Charles said.

"And afterwards?"

Charles grinned. "That is something which will arrange itself."

"And what are you posing as?"

"I am a chauffeur-valet. Everyone has the possibilities of a valet, and I also can drive a car. Like that, one should be safe." He gave one of his roguish looks. "I also have a fear of the police. Besides the affair of last night, there was a something else of which I am now about to work out the details."

Whatever the faint lingerings of indignation, Travers could no longer regard with serious disapproval that insinuation of Charles into the confidences of Elise Deschamps. Phrases like not playing the game, and not cricket, seemed very British and very much claptrap when one considered that the woman was doubtless only too capable of looking after her own interests, and that Charles himself was regarding the adventure with a cynical amusement. And Gallois had certainly been right. To each country its own methods, and it was for *messieurs les assassins* to commence wearing kid gloves.

He stayed for a final word with Cointeau. Had anyone at any time come in especially to see Braque? Anyone that might be now regarded as a criminal associate?

Cointeau said there was no one. Then he recalled a someone on the morning of the murder, and from the description, Travers recognized Henri Larne. The account given by Cointeau tallied exactly with that which Larne himself had given of those guarded enquiries he had made about Braque, and Travers made no comment. Then he requested the use of the phone, and rang the Sûreté. A call from Travers had been expected, and the Inspector, he was told, would be ready for him in half an hour.

The room was empty when Travers was shown in, but on the desk were those two atrocities in paint. Travers was having another look at them when Gallois came in. A melancholy smile was hovering about his lips, and his hand was held out.

"A thousand felicitations, my friend. All this beneath our eyes, and it is you who make the discovery."

Travers said modestly it was no credit of his. He suffered from the curse of a tidy mind, and a mystery or even a peculiarity would no more let him rest than would thistles in his bed.

"I should have known," Gallois said, and shook his head despondently. "One does not keep atrocities without reason. But while we know that Braque was this picture smuggler whom we suspected, there is too much in which we remain in the dark. I hear from M. Schiffler that the pictures were undoubtedly removed from Spain, but I also know that the pictures which you have discovered are already for six months behind these frames."

"You've had a report already?"

"To me it was essential that I should know at once. I am not here when you arrive because I await the report. Now that we know, we know also something else. Instead of being nearer to the moment when we apprehend the assassin, we are much farther away."

Travers smiled. "My dear Gallois, you're not telling me that it's done us harm to discover Braque's gold-mine?"

The lean fingers of Gallois were clawing the air impatiently.

"Listen, my friend, and I explain. Months ago Braque mentions a gold-mine. It is then that he has his trip to Spain, and he brings back pictures which he conceals in the frames of those two atrocities. But the gold-mine is an affair of the most disappointing. He cannot dispose of the pictures and he makes therefore no more visits to Spain. And he confesses to the good Cointeau that it is a failure, this mine.

"But a few weeks ago he mentions that *second* mine. And it is a mine of a character altogether different. For example, it produces dividends. Moreover, it leads to a knife in his ribs, and, my friend, one does not receive a knife in the ribs because of pictures from Spain: pictures which still remain concealed behind the atrocities."

Travers mentioned what Cointeau had let fall that very afternoon about Braque's gold-mine.

"I see it like this," he said. "More than one person must have been concerned in the picture smuggling. Isn't that so?"

Gallois suavely agreed.

"The scheme fell through," went on Travers. "It lay dormant just as those pictures lay dormant inside those two frames. That was the end of the first gold-mine. But then Braque thought of another method of approach, and he was so sure of its success that he thought of it—and so described it to Cointeau—as a *second* gold-mine, even though it was only a modification of the first.

"The scheme, I believe, was this: that he should find private buyers in England for those pictures. As a means of introduction he decided to use the name of Larne. He therefore made some study of Larne's pictures, in order to be able to answer questions, and—remember this—he didn't want to buy any Larnes. He merely hinted at a possible client in the future. The reason he chose the name of Larne was that he was with him at the Académie Poussin, which would sound very convincing."

"He mentioned to you in London this Académie Poussin?"

"No," said Travers ruefully. "That was one of his trump cards to be used only in case of necessity. He regarded me as so very likely a victim that he hadn't need to play his trumps."

"Very well," said Gallois. "Let us admit all this. But how does it bring us nearer to the assassin of this Braque?"

"In this way," Travers told him. "The first gold-mine had failed, and the associates of Braque were becoming anxious. They began to think he was playing some double game, and it was one of them who killed him. For instance, this one who killed him—our assassin, in fact—became aware that Braque had money, and he drew the only possible conclusion—that Braque had double-crossed the gang."

"Then one commences all over again—"

The buzzer went at his elbow, and he picked up the receiver.

"Good," he said, and repeated the word with a nod of satisfaction. "Ask him to have the goodness to wait for five minutes only."

His smile, as he turned to Travers, was so less mournful that it almost amounted to the hilarious.

"At last something arrives. It is not much, but it is something. Already I have ascertained who it is that are the acquaintances of Braque, and this afternoon I interrogate them here. But they are acquaintances and not—what you say?—partners in crime. They know nothing of his private affairs; even this good Olivier, who is the picture framer for the firm. But it emerges that this Olivier was with Braque until just before he was murdered. In order to exonerate himself, he makes, at my suggestion, certain enquiries. I go now to see what it is that he has discovered. Without doubt you wish to come also?"

"Without the slightest doubt," smiled Travers, and got at once to his feet.

CHAPTER IX
TRAVERS IS PUZZLED

WHAT TRAVERS WAS SOON to gather was this. The firm of Olivier which did the picture framing for Braque and Cointeau, had their shop within a hundred yards of Braque's shop, but it was at the Café Wagram, some way along the Boulevard Bastide, where Braque and Olivier used to meet. But not necessarily on business. The meetings were rather of that sociable quality, at the accustomed hour of five o'clock, and there was a small circle which would assemble for an early aperitif and a chat.

On the afternoon of Braque's murder, only three of the friends came to the Café Wagram, and just before half-past five, Braque and Olivier were left alone. At half-past Braque suddenly caught sight of the time and said he would have to fly. A quick handshake, and he was hailing a taxi.

Gallois had put two men at the disposal of Olivier, and it was the taxi-driver who was waiting at the Café Wagram. He confirmed that it was at half-past five that he had picked up the fare, who had said he was in a great hurry. Then something rather strange happened. The taxi was held up, and the driver turned to Braque and protested that the fault was not his. Braque, who had been in such a hurry, now shrugged his shoulders, and he made use of an extraordinary phrase which the driver insisted was: "Let the bastard wait!"

The implications were obvious. At the rue Jourdoise Braque was meeting somebody whom he would have liked to meet on time, but on the other hand he had so little respect for that somebody that he was indifferent whether or not he waited in the cold and drizzle outside the flat door. Braque had most certainly therefore not gone to the flat to meet Travers.

Gallois thanked Olivier and had a last word with him. He was still sure that Braque had received no telephone message at the café? Olivier was positive. He had been in Braque's company for the half-hour and Braque had never left his seat.

"And how long was it that your vehicle was held up?" Gallois asked the driver.

"Five minutes, perhaps," he said. "After that one travels quick, and one regains a minute."

"Drive us to where you set the fare down," Gallois said, "and try to travel at the same speed. It is I who will make allowances for the wait."

It was about a hundred metres short of the rue Jourdoise that the driver stopped. Gallois made the time nine minutes in all. Then, when the driver was dismissed, he began walking towards Braque's flat.

"It will be better to talk there," he said. "One has there the atmosphere, and for those of the sensibility of ourselves that is an essential, is it not?"

A gendarme was still on duty at the back stairs. The flat struck damp and chill, and the living-room seemed curiously more bare without those two garish pictures. Gallois lit the gas stove. Travers, feeling somewhat leg-weary, took a chair. Gallois prowled restlessly about the room.

"You're still not happy about things?" Travers said.

Gallois anchored himself for a minute or two by Travers's chair.

"One does not arrive yet at the moment in which to be happy. But we achieve something that is not without interest. At five-forty Braque arrives here, and, unhappily, it is before I myself arrive. He admits the assassin, with whom he has the rendezvous, or perhaps the assassin admits himself, and kills Braque over there, when he enters. The assassin takes money, papers, everything and at once he is gone." He raised hands of exasperation. "He had luck, that one. Five minutes later and we should have followed him."

"And where does this get us to?"

Gallois came back again.

"Gently, my friend. It is necessary to think slowly. But it is not you that Braque comes here to meet. I tell you that before, on account of the shaving. Now also there are other ideas it is necessary to change. One does not telephone Braque to come in a hurry to the flat. All the day, perhaps, he knows that he will meet the assassin here. And therefore, my friend, you are not concerned at all."

"But I *was* concerned," insisted Travers. "Haven't we agreed that the assassin arranged for me to meet Braque here at six o'clock?"

Gallois smiled patiently. "One admits that, but consider. The assassin—this man who knows your hotel, and your affairs, and who speaks no English— he arranges that he himself comes here at a quarter of an hour before, and he knows that by then Braque will be dead. Why then should he also arrange with Braque to see you here at six o'clock?"

But Travers was whipping off his glasses.

"I know! Braque hadn't the faintest idea I was coming here. It was the assassin who wanted me here, to implicate me in the murder. He didn't have the least idea that I had been to you."

Gallois was prowling round the room again. Once more he slowed up by Travers's chair.

"But an assassin who knows your affairs, knows also that one like yourself cannot be long suspected of murder. One makes enquiries, and *voilà*. There is perhaps another reason why you should come here?"

"I've got it!" Travers said. "It was so that I should discover the body. The assassin knew me well enough to know that I should at once inform the police. They would know when Braque was killed. They'd know it to a minute—"

"Precisely!" Gallois was not to be robbed of his own share of credit. "The assassin wished that we discover that Braque is killed at a quarter to six, *because he has arranged for himself an alibi for a quarter to six.*"

"Exactly. But why so despondent?"

"I am not despondent," protested Gallois. "I am unquiet. Even if one discovers this assassin—of what use? If he establishes the alibi, it is no good that you and I know that without doubt he is the assassin."

"We'll jump that obstacle when we arrive at it," Travers told him confidently. "But have you any suspicions yourself?"

"Who is the assassin?" He shook his head. "There is the good Cointeau who still does not emerge, as you say, from the wood. One still does not discover the client who confirms his alibi."

"But why abandon my original suggestion— Pierre Larne?"

But at the very same second, while he waited for the answer of Gallois, he had the sudden idea that something was being concealed. Why should Gallois possibly have any suspicion of Cointeau? How could Cointeau possibly have known the Paris address and Travers's affairs, unless he were hand in glove with his dead partner? And that implied that the simple, obvious

Cointeau was a murderer of the most cunning type, and the world's supreme actor as well.

"Pierre Larne," Gallois was saying. "You perhaps have discovered something new?"

Travers was in an awkward position, as he explained. Larne had made certain confidences which he could not divulge.

"I can tell you this much," he said. "Pierre is the parasite you described him, and Henri is breaking with him. I sympathize with Henri. He's got a woman there looking after him, and her husband is ill, and I rather suspect some underhand goings-on between her and Pierre, so that altogether Henri hasn't had the atmosphere he requires for work. Now this woman and her husband are going away, and I rather fancy the Villa will be sold."

"Yes, but, my friend, why should we suspect this Pierre when you already assure me he has an alibi."

Travers smiled suggestively. "Didn't I hint that there might be underhand work going on? It's the woman, Hortense, who's the mainstay of the alibi. Also I'm betraying no confidences when I say that Henri suspects that Pierre is lying about the whole thing."

Gallois shook his head. "These restrictions are difficult, not that I blame you, my friend. But is it not possible that you should at least hint something more?"

"Well, I'll give you my ideas for what they're worth," Travers said. "I think Pierre was a member of the Braque gang. I suspect him of purloining his half-brother's works, and I believe Henri is hushing the matter up. There, by the way, is another reason why Braque, as the seller, showed an interest in Larne's work. And I may tell you that when I undid the back of the first of those pictures this afternoon, I expected to find some inferior work of Larne's concealed behind it."

"In Henri Larne I am not interested," pronounced Gallois. "He was of interest if he could explain to us the connection between his pictures and Braque. Now that is perhaps explained, he ceases to interest us as far as concerns the assassin of Braque.

But Pierre, he is different. The alibi does not matter provided we can prove some association with Braque. It is possible that the woman Moulins may reveal something."

"Moulins?" Travers had forgotten the name.

"The woman Deschamps, whose real name is Moulins. If not, we may even confront her with this Pierre to see if she recognizes, but at the moment I would not resort to that. Through his brother he doubtless has influence, and it is necessary that I should give reasons to my superiors before advancing so far."

"The Académie Poussin; mightn't we get some possible information there about Braque?" suggested Travers.

"That exists no longer," Gallois said, "but I am on the point of finding a certain Professeur Tagnier who visited there at the time of Braque. There is a business, my friend, with which you might employ yourself."

Travers said he would be delighted to take on that much when the information arrived. Meanwhile, what?

"For the moment we rest," Gallois told him. "There comes always a moment when it is necessary to think, and not employ one's self. To-morrow perhaps we occupy ourselves with this Pierre."

Then his hand fell on Travers's shoulder and he was smiling affectionately.

"Before this affair is over, you will perhaps be very displeased with me."

"Good heavens, why?"

"That is something which I cannot say, but you will see that it becomes true."

Travers shook his head. "Don't you believe it. What interests me more is to hear you talk about the affair being over."

"Soon—very soon, perhaps—it will be over," Gallois said. "One more discovery like that which you make to-day, and we lay our hands on the assassins of Braque. You remember that I speak to you of the resemblance most strange that exists between me and M. Larne? Now there is something else that occurs to me. You tell me that M. Larne, he desires quiet for his work and he takes an action which is drastic and disembarrasses himself of everything. Soon also, my friend, we take our-selves an action which is drastic, though I do not know precisely when that moment arrives."

"I'm glad to hear it," Travers said, puzzled though he was.

The hand of Gallois fell on his shoulder again.

"One other thing, my friend. M. Lame has finished to-day what is a masterpiece. This affair"—his lean fingers turned in-wards to his breast— "and I feel it in the soul of me, will also be a masterpiece. The masterpiece of Gallois, and of you also, my friend."

He was staying behind for some minutes, he said, in that place which was so congenial to his thoughts, and Travers walked back to the hotel in the dear frosty air of the February night. But his own thoughts were far from clear, and he found himself no part of those optimisms of Gallois.

"All these people are strange to me," he told himself. "Even Gallois, well, as I know him and much as I like him, remains something different. Perhaps inability to speak their language fluently has something to do with it, but whatever it is, there's always that feeling of not quite getting beneath their hides. Charles, for instance, one of the most attractive young fellows I've ever run across, and yet I can't feel that I really know him. Then there was that scene at the Villa this morning, with Henri Larne and Pierre and that Hortense woman, and the squabbling, and the queer sort of undercurrent which you felt but couldn't place. Still, perhaps the case is tying me down too much and getting on my nerves. Gallois keeps hinting at things I don't see, and maybe he's right. And that last hint of his was right too. There's a time in every case when it's good to lay off for a bit and do a little stocktaking instead."

So when Travers woke the next morning he resolved to take things easy, and hold back till Gallois rang or appeared. Then soon after ten o'clock there was a ring, but it was from Henri Larne. He would esteem it a favour if Travers could come along for only a minute or two. Travers thought it unnecessary to inform Gallois of his whereabouts for so brief a time and set off at once.

At the Villa a small van was being packed with luggage, and Larne himself was supervising the loading of the pictures. He looked ten years younger than when Travers had seen him last.

"The moving's beginning, then?" Travers said.

"Most of it's over," Larne told him triumphantly. "I'm the only one left and these are the last of my things."

"You're going too?"

"Only to the Hôtel Coutance. But come upstairs. There's something I want you to do for me."

Travers refused so early a drink but accepted a cigarette. Larne had switched on the fire, and they sat talking for a few minutes about plans.

"Hortense and her husband have gone already this morning," Larne said. "She has a sister near Grenoble and the air ought to do the husband good. Pierre is seeing to everything." He smiled, but not too unkindly. "As it is the last function he performs for me for some time, he ought to do it satisfactorily. Almost at once I shall sell this place and everything in it. Which reminds me. I had a proposition yesterday from the American collector—a very charming man, by the way, and I'd have liked you to meet him. He suggests that I should go to America for a time."

"But how delightful for you!" Travers said. "You think you'll go."

"I promised to send him a cable on his arrival," Larne said, and seemed somewhat amused. "What he does not know is that I was there some years ago. I told you, if you remember, that when I saw no prospects here, I threw everything up and became a rolling stone—" He broke off with a wave of the hand. "That all belongs to the past. If I thought the creative impulses would be stimulated, I might try the experiment again."

"If you'll pardon me," Travers said, "you might paint more, but I doubt if you'd paint better."

"That's more than generous of you," Larne told him quietly. "But I feel I'm going to do both. I'm what you might call free for the first time for years." He was suddenly getting to his feet. "But about this something I want you to do for me. I can rely on you?"

"I hope so."

"Then it's this." Travers had not noticed the smallish picture that had stood near them with its back to the wall, and now it was being put in his hands. "Accept this from me, as what one calls a small token of esteem."

Travers stared. "But, my dear fellow, I couldn't."

"Why not?"

"Well"—he smiled lamely—"I've done nothing. Even if I had, the gift is out of all proportion. One day this will be exceedingly valuable."

Larne shrugged his shoulders. "That, if you pardon me, I don't agree with. It's merely a study, as you see. Some people would work on it, but that's not my way. I regarded it as what it is, and I've finished with it."

The study was of a small table with a coloured cloth, on which stood an empty blue vase. The marguerites which lay by it were scarcely painted at all, yet even their charcoal stalks showed a perfection of placing. Travers liked the little study enormously and made no bones about admitting it.

"I hate to appear churlish," he said, "but what on earth have I done to merit this marvellous present?"

"You honoured me with your confidences," Larne said quietly. "Not only that. If I hadn't also confided in you, I should never have painted that last picture. You didn't know it, but you changed my whole outlook. I might even say it's thanks to you that I've plucked up courage to rid myself of various encumbrances. That was what I thought this morning when Pierre's car went off, and as soon as I knew it, I knew what I was going to do and I rang you up."

"I accept the picture only too gratefully, then," Travers said. "I still know I don't in any way deserve it."

He was still shaking his head diffidently, and Larne was watching him with quiet amusement.

"That's all right, then," he said. "And now I'm hurrying you away before you change your mind."

"Yes, of course," Travers said. "You must be very busy."

"And you? You're busy too?"

"I'm merely a potterer," Travers said. "Gallois is a very old friend of mine and I'm doing my best to help find out who murdered that scoundrel Braque. We've definitely found a connection, by the way, between him and that picture smuggling from Spain, but I'll tell you about it some time later."

He smiled and he remembered something else.

"I've promised to do something which might interest you. I shall probably be making enquiries from some old professor or other about Braque when he was at the Académie Poussin—now defunct, I believe."

Larne halted, puzzledly.

"But why make enquiries there?"

Travers's shrug of the shoulders was perfect Gallic.

"We suspect a ring of these smugglers. Why shouldn't one at least of Braque's confederates have been some old friend of his? A contemporary at the Academy, for instance."

Larne chuckled, and he was waving his hands with all the excited pleasure of remembrance.

"The Académie Poussin—what a place! Only about a dozen of us there in my time, and what a collection!" He shook his head. "There was Braque, fat and very unpleasant, and paying other people to do his work. Then there was a tall, lean fellow called—called—oh yes, called Letori. I could tell you the most scandalous story about him. Then there was a man called Moulins, who was undoubtedly mad. Used to drink like—"

"Moulins! A Moulins who used to drink?"

"Why, yes," said Larne, staring in his turn. "Did you know him, then?"

"No," said Travers. "But we're up against a most amazing co-incidence. You remember that model—Elise Deschamps—who was posing for you? Her real name is Moulins. Her father drank himself to death and her brother too. Both were artists."

Larne's face had gone pale and he seemed to be in the grip of some tremendous perturbation. A moment or two and he let out a breath, and was shaking his head bewilderingly.

"It's uncanny," he said. "I was the one who used to befriend that Moulins, and give him advice and try to pull him together. And there's something else. Something about the other night."

He was nodding gently to himself as he thought. Then he shook his head with a quick finality.

"No, I can't tell you yet. But an idea occurs to me."

"To do with the murder of Braque?"

"That I can't tell you. I must have time to think. Perhaps I am wrong. I must he wrong."

His hand was all at once gripping Travers's arm.

"You will say nothing of this. It is dangerous to have a suspicion and not be able to substantiate it."

"I quite agree," Travers said. "There is only one thing. You owe a duty to the law, and as soon as your suspicion is more than a suspicion—and, by the way, I haven't the faintest notion myself what it is you're suspicious about—then you should inform Gallois at once."

"I agree." He nodded to himself determinedly, "in a few days, perhaps, I shall be sure. In the meanwhile we'll forget all about it. All this business has pressed on my mind till it has driven me nearly crazy. Not this *affaire* Braque—that is nothing— though there also I have certain suspicions."

"As you say, we'll forget it," Travers told him consolingly. "What you need, my dear fellow, is to get away from here and have a good rest at your hotel."

Downstairs again, Larne recovered most of his good humour, and he waved a cheery hand as Travers's taxi drove off. Travers had yet another mystery on his mind. That morning he had woke remembering that queer statement that Gallois had made, that before the case was finished with, he, Travers, would be very annoyed. What that meant Travers had no idea, and now, not only was there that coincidence of the brother of Elise at the Académie Poussin, but—and Travers had no doubts, startling though the deduction was—there was Larne now of the opinion that Elise had been concerned in the murder of Braque. *Concerned in it*—that was all it could be, for Larne himself knew only too well that Elise could never have committed the actual murder.

At the first opportunity Travers stopped the taxi and rang up Gallois.

"You are fortunate," Gallois said, "for I am this moment about, to go. But there is something which you do not understand?"

"I don't follow you. What do you mean?"

"You are not speaking from your hotel?"

"No," said Travers. "Larne rang me up, as I told you, and I've just been to see him. What I happened to discover was that the brother of the woman Moulins was at the Académie Poussin with Braque."

There was a moment's silence, then: "You are, sure?"

"Absolutely sure."

"Then listen also to this, my friend. You return now to your hotel and you find two surprises. One I will tell you now. It is that the woman Moulins proves that Pierre Larne was also an acquaintance of Braque."

CHAPTER X
GALLOIS MAKES A MOVE

TRAVERS CAME literally bounding into the private sitting-room at the hotel. Bernice was reading before the fire.

"I got back much earlier than I thought," she said. "And what on earth is that? You haven't been buying pictures?"

Travers, tearing off the wrappings, explained. The picture was placed for Bernice's inspection.

"Now I must say I like that," she said. "It may be only a study as you say, but I do like it very much indeed. And the little flying donkey in the corner and all."

"Larne is a queer chap," Travers was saying, face still alight with the pleasure of that picture. "A really famous man and yet as unaffected as a nobody. If ever you make me write that book of reminiscences—"

"Oh!" broke in Bernice, and a rather strained look came over her face. "I ought to have told you that the valet has come."

"The valet!"

Bernice explained with a patience that only too obviously shielded a grievance.

"The young man you thought might suit you as a valet."

"What on earth *is* this? Why should I want a valet?"

"That's just what I wondered," Bernice said.

Then Travers was staring again.

"Where is he?"

"In the anteroom," Bernice said, with something of the same faint frigidity. "He said he was to wait."

Travers, with visions of thieves and false pretences, was already across the room and opening the door.

"Charles! What the devil are you doing here?"

"I came to offer my services as valet," Charles said in the most careful and laborious English.

"Come in here," Travers told him. "Bernice, this is Charles, whom you've heard me mention. This is some joke or other—"

"You permit," broke in Charles, in the same careful English. "It is not a joke, but it is serious. I come actually to demand if monsieur wishes a valet. I am a good valet and I conduct also a car."

Travers chuckled. The eyes of Charles caught those of Bernice and she had to smile too.

"I'll leave you to get out of the muddle for yourselves," she said.

Charles was across the room in a flash and opening the door for her. Then Travers had him by the arm and was leading him to a chair.

"Now let's hear what all this is about. What the devil do you mean by coming here and posing to my wife as a valet?"

Charles shrugged his shoulders and appeared not to be amused.

"I assure you, monsieur, that it is serious. What actually happens is this."

As Charles related those experiences of the last few hours the most strange of illusions began to take possession of the mind of Travers. There was the slow, pleasant voice of the young *agent,* his friendly face, and his smile that had much of the sad, brooding quality of Gallois. So simply and so convincingly did he describe things, that it was as if he really had become that wholly new person in whose guise he had made the acquaintance of Elise. She too became something intensely personal, so that Travers had the queer feeling of listening to some intimate and indeed moving tragedy, that belonged to no tinselled, artificial Bohemia of the stage. It was the story of flesh and blood; of two human beings, drawn together by loneliness and misfortune, and finding suddenly a need of each other, and a consolation in misfortune itself.

Charles had waited some time at the rendezvous the previous night, for Elise was late. When she arrived she was still very distressed. At the morning's chance meeting she had given a version of her relations with Braque, and now she confided that the police had taken her to the Morgue to identify the body, and had also questioned her, though she knew nothing.

The two went to a little restaurant for a meal, and Charles too was indignant against the police. There was a false charge which had been brought against him by a former employer, and yet the police would still not leave him alone. And, of course, there was that business of the previous night, though he doubted if he'd be recognized again after the darkness of the rue de Jourdoise.

The intimacy of that meal, and even their own whispered voices, brought a sympathy, and soon she was telling him how she had met Braque. She had been hard-up at the time and it was he who had proposed things. She was desperate and accepted his arrangements, but when she saw the apartment he was providing, she had a sudden revulsion of feeling and refused to have anything to do with the affair.

"You were lucky," Charles said, indicating the headline in the paper he had just bought. "One does not deal sympathetically with the friends of swine like this Braque."

That was what was frightening her, she said. The police would not believe her, and if anything got out about herself, her livelihood might be affected. Charles asked why she did not seek the aid of relations or friends, and then she was telling him more about herself: the terrifying crazy existence with her father and brother, with squalor and rows and embroilments with the police. There was one fight between the pair, when the brother was slashed across the mouth with a knife, and when he came out of hospital, he was away for some time, no one knew where. Then the father died, and the brother went on with his career as an artist. Then he began to show signs of the same madness and ultimately he disappeared. All this, as she related it, was against the background of Paris during the war, and an atmosphere that in itself was crazy and unreal.

Then she changed her name and found work as a model, and from then—mere child though she was—she had managed to support herself in that precarious profession. Then, only five years ago, she had received through an old friend, now dead, a letter from a priest in Algiers, telling her of the death of her brother there.

It was a tragic history, and yet the history of Charles—and it was a true history, as he assured Travers—had something in common. He also was an orphan, and had been brought up by a grand-mother, and ultimately a patron had interested himself and found him work. Now he was seeking a new job and finding it heart-breaking. But one always had hopes and one continued to exist in spite of everything.

The couple read that evening paper together, with its news of the *affaire* Braque, and lingered out their time till the opening of the cinema. There they sat close in the warm dark, and soon were once more whispering together about themselves. Charles was finding it inexplicable that the police had not accepted her statements. Had she by any chance become involved, without then being aware of it, in those schemes the paper had mentioned? Or with any of the friends of Braque? But she knew no friends of Braque, she said. She even knew nothing in reality about Braque himself, except that at first he had been kind, and had spent his money.

They walked by dark deserted side-streets to the rue Vagnolles, where Charles said good night. She asked where he was going, and he said to Belleville, where he had a room. She insisted that he should come in first and drink something warm, for he was shivering after the warmth of the cinema and he had no overcoat.

She had two small rooms above a derelict garage. The kitchen was also the living-room, and there was a tiny bedroom. She heated coffee for them both and they sat talking once more about themselves. Soon she was remembering something. There *was* a friend of Braque whom she had seen. Twice she had seen him. Once, about a fortnight ago, she was with Braque at a restaurant and this Pierre appeared. She did not know his other name, but the description she gave was Pierre Larne to the life. At the sight of him Braque had abruptly paid the bill and had left her, and joined him. Later that week she had seen the two in the same restaurant, their heads together in talk.

Charles said something would have to be done. If one knew more, one could understand the persecution of the police, and one could make one's plans. But it was late, and he rose to go. But there was no need for him to go all that way to a cold room, she said. He could occupy the kitchen, and she would find him clothes. He would not hear of it, but she insisted, and he finally agreed.

So he slept that night on the kitchen floor, and she occupied the bedroom. He slept soundly, he said, and it was not till dawn that he woke. Then the door opened and she appeared, already dressed. "Now you take the bed." she said, "and rest there till I am ready. I have affairs to see to."

From the warm bed he could hear her washing at the kitchen tap, and then she went out. In half an hour she was back, and soon there was the smell of coffee. She brought the little breakfast to his room, and he asked where he could wash and shave.

"There is time for that," she said. "This morning I do not work, and you also have no need of hurry."

"You are good," he said. "When I obtain this work, there are perhaps things I shall do for you."

"It is you who are good," she said. "When one is a model, one meets all types, and one learns. Me, I am nothing but what I am, but you are different."

Once more they were talking about themselves. What he would like, he said, was to get into the employment of some Englishman. They paid well and were good masters.

There was an Englishman, she said. He was a friend of the great painter Larne, and she told him all the story of how he had returned to the villa, and how later he had either gone or been taken to the rue Jourdoise with herself.

"He is rich, this Englishman?" Charles asked her.

She did not know, she said, but he had that air.

"Then he has already a valet-chauffeur," he said. "Perhaps he has both."

Then he also remembered something. If the Englishman had been with Gallois and at Braque's flat, then doubtless he knew many things about the police. If one could enter his service, one also could doubtless learn many things. But where did this Englishman live?

But that, unhappily, she did not know, and Charles himself could only shrug his shoulders helplessly. Then he remembered something. One had only to make enquiries among the taxi-drivers, and many were his friends, and he would discover where the Englishman had been driven. All that was needed was a description.

Almost at once he was shaving, and Elise herself brushed his clothes and cleaned his boots.

Abruptly, and yet aptly, the story ended. Something of the illusion had already gone, and yet Travers hardly knew.

"And you return this evening to her apartment?" he said.

"Yes," said Charles quietly, "I return."

Travers shook his head. "While you were telling me what you'd been doing, I could almost believe you were what you said you were."

Charles looked astonished.

"But, monsieur, I *am* what I say I am. In order to convince others, it is necessary at first to convince one's self. And my story was true. I am an orphan who never knew father or mother. For the rest—" and he shrugged his shoulders.

"And you have changed your mind about this Elise?"

"But, how?"

Travers explained somewhat diffidently. His own idea had been that she was no better than a considerable number of her kind.

"But one knows all that," Charles said. "If monsieur permits me to recall the fact, she explains that herself. When one is a model, one must prepare to meet all the types. It is necessary to arm one's self with a certain knowledge of affairs, and even a pretended vulgarity. But at heart she is also different."

Travers shrugged his shoulders.

"So long as this comedy that you play remains a comedy, everything will be well. This evening you may announce that you have seen the Englishman, who has given you employment while he remains here in Paris. This evening, perhaps, you celebrate. And now let's forget romance and come back to hard facts. Do you know what M. Gallois is doing about the information you were able to give him—that Pierre Larne was a friend of Braque?"

Charles said he was once more making enquiries at the bureau of the models. It was absolutely necessary to know how it was that Elise had been the model to be sent to the Villa Claire. If it was she herself who had contrived it, then things would have to be looked at from a different angle, especially in view of the information that Pierre Larne and Braque had been associates.

"Then you do not believe her?" asked the astonished Travers.

"It is necessary to make sure," Charles said. "Also it is not what I believe. It is what M. Gallois believes." He shrugged his shoulders. "Where women are concerned, he is not sympathetic, that one."

Then he remembered that he had a note from his chief. It merely told Travers that Gallois was making enquiries in certain directions, and meanwhile would Travers go to a Fontainebleau address which Charles knew, and interview M. le Professeur Frigot, and obtain any information about Braque as the Professor knew him.

"Then we go to Fontainebleau," Travers said to Charles. "But there is no mention of hurry."

"You permit that I say something?" Charles said. "Since I am now in the service of monsieur, to-night or to-morrow it will be necessary to hire an auto. I also must procure myself some clothes."

"No time like the present," Travers told him dryly. "You obtain your clothes and I obtain the auto. At fourteen hours we start, which allows time for lunch. Then in half an hour we should be at Fontainebleau."

Charles smiled like his old happy-go-lucky self for the first time since entering that room.

"That, monsieur, depends on the auto."

Travers drove the hired car—an English limousine which its former owner had exchanged for a French car—and Charles told him what was known about the Académie Poussin. It had been nothing of the size or importance of the famous Julien, not had it been situated in the neighbourhood of the Sorbonne, and yet in its own way it had had a considerable vogue before the War, chiefly owing to the reputation of its visiting professors.

Frigot, now a very old man, was apparently one of the last of these, and with a garrulity of age he insisted on recounting to Travers his own contacts with the great figures of the end of the century. Then at last Travers got him pinned down to the defunct Académie Poussin, already in decay when Frigot first knew it. All he would talk about then was Henri Larne, a student of curious temper, as he described him, but misplaced as a portrait painter, as time had shown. Frigot professed to have foreseen that Larne would one day be a somebody. There was a portrait of his, he said, which had been exhibited at one of the minor galleries, and which gave the critics a chance too good to be missed, and he remembered how for the first time there was that obvious and nevertheless insulting play upon his name, and a recommendation to the donkey to confine itself to its thistles.

"And now the donkey flies," smiled Travers.

The old man chuckled delightedly.

"Monsieur knows, I see. The donkey indeed flies, and it is the critics who remain on the ground with their thistles."

Braque he also remembered. He was heavy and stodgy in his work, but inclined to give himself airs. Frigot had informed him that he would never earn a flea's keep with his brush.

And so to the other students, and it was Travers who had to recall a certain Moulins.

"Ah!" said the old man excitedly. "There indeed was a curiosity."

He elaborated with much gesture. A painter of extreme brilliance who could accomplish with a turn of the brush what the idiots failed to do in hours. But a madman undoubtedly. Ditty, unkempt, and one who already consumed too many glasses. There was drink and madness in the family. Frigot had slightly known the father, who might also have become a somebody but for himself.

"Wasn't there a daughter?" asked Travers.

That he did not remember, but there was much more he had to tell of Moulins.

"You know, perhaps, *L'Homme Qui Rit* of Victor Hugo? The jester whose mouth was cut so that he appeared always to smile? That was this Moulins. In an accident his face was cut, and he had an air so comical that he was the butt of the students. It. was that which doubtless embittered him." He shook his head. "Then I cease to go to the Academic, and later I enquire for this one and that, and I am told of him that he has left and where he is no one knows. Until you speak of him to-day, I do not hear his name."

"He's dead now," Travers said. "He died in Algiers five years ago."

The old man nodded to himself at the news, and was silent for a moment or two. Then he said that Moulins had doubtless become a species of Gauguin and had been living a hand-to-mouth existence in the colonies. He had known several like that, he said, and then was at once away on a dissertation on the perils of the artistic temperament.

It was almost dusk when Travers arrived back at the hotel. Arrangements had already been made to park the car at the garage where it had been hired. Travers wrote a note for Gallois, saying that no new information had emerged, and he was proposing to remain at the hotel and at the Inspector's disposal.

"You're going afterwards to the apartment of Elise?" Travers asked Charles, who was to deliver the note.

"First, with the permission of monsieur, I will change my clothes here," Charles said.

"You're not going to display yourself?"

Charles shook his head.

"In these affairs, monsieur, it is necessary that one should move slowly. To-night I announce merely that I am under consideration by monsieur, and it will be to-morrow that he engages me and I obtain the clothes."

"Perhaps you're right," said Travers, and smiled. "It is not only M. Gallois who is an artist."

"When one is *chez les artistes*, it is necessary that one becomes an artist one's self," said the enigmatic Charles, and disappeared into the cloakroom to effect his changing.

As Travers watched the door close on him, he had once again that queer feeling of being on the outside of things. For the young *agent* he was beginning to have something like affection, and yet with him, as with Gallois, there was a queer something somewhere, like a door that is opened to reveal a view that one admires and likes, and then without reason is closed again.

Then Bernice arrived home, and was told all the news. Travers forgot all about the *affaire* Braque for at least an hour. It was, in fact, at six o'clock that the hotel phone informed him that a M. Gallois desired most urgently to see him at the bureau. Travers grabbed hat and coat and fairly sprinted down the stairs.

"Ah, my friend," said Gallois, and shook him warmly by the hand.

Then he was leading him off to a deserted corner of the lounge, and he refused Travers's offer of a drink.

"There isn't even a minute that we can spare," he said. "But it is at the Hôtel Coutance, is it not, that M. Lame has removed to-day?"

Once more it was as if the door had closed. For the life of him Travers could not help but know that Gallois was only too well aware of the name of Larne's hotel.

"That was the name," he said. "But I don't know if he's actually moved in there yet."

"It is not M. Larne himself that I wish," Gallois said, "except that he gives information perhaps about this brother who is an associate of Braque. At that bureau of the models, I expect to find news of the brother, but there was none. To them he is unknown."

"And the model Élise?"

"Everything was as she tells us," Gallois said. "She arrives at the bureau and she is sent to the Villa. There is only one thing. That woman at the bureau. There is something which says she does not tell the truth." He made a gesture of indifference. "But that does not matter. It is this Pierre Larne whom it is necessary that we see."

"But you won't be able to see him," pointed out Travers. "I think I told you that he's taking the two servants to an aunt of theirs at Grenoble. He started early this morning, but he wouldn't do the journey in a day."

Gallois made another gesture of indifference.

"Nevertheless, my friend, perhaps you will do me the favour of demanding M. Larne on the phone, and requesting an interview of only five minutes for yourself. There is no need to mention my name. Meanwhile I will perhaps drink the apéritif you have the goodness to offer."

Travers was fortunate in his telephoning. In five minutes he was back. M. Larne would see him at once.

"Then we go at once," Gallois said, "and it is I who will explain my arrival. And there is one tiling of which I must advise you, my friend. You will hear perhaps some things that astonish. Retain, nevertheless, I beg of you, a composure even when they are things which astonish. And leave here at the bureau a note for madame your wife, that tonight you return late." He thought for a moment. "There is even a possibility that you do not return at all."

CHAPTER XI
THE HOUSE ON THE DUNES

GALLOIS HAD a fast, powerful car, with a special driver, and in less than five minutes they were at Larne's hotel.

"Remember that it is I who will speak," Gallois whispered as they stepped out of the life. "I also will explain how it is that I am here myself."

Travers rang and it was Larne who opened the door.

"I've brought a visitor," Travers said, "and he's going to explain himself."

Larne's look had been curiously watchful, but now he smiled too, though the smile was forced and wary.

"Come in, please. It's nothing serious, I hope?"

"It is nothing at all," Gallois said, and in English. "I go to the hotel of M. Travers, and he decides that it is best that we see you. It is about your brother."

"My brother?" His eyes narrowed, then he made a gesture of indifference. "But sic down. And what may I offer you to drink?"

"At the moment, nothing," Travers said. Gallois refused too, being, as he said, in a great hurry. "We do not wish to take your so valuable time," Gallois explained. "But what arrives is that M. Travers is a friend of you and of me also. There are confidences that you make to him, and when it is necessary that I question him, he refuses as a man of honour to divulge the confidences that you make. Therefore I say that we must come to you." His shrug of the shoulders was almost abject. "I do not wish that you make confidences to me, but there are things which I say it is necessary for you to know."

Larne smiled, if somewhat ironically.

"Well, what are these things that I ought to know?"

"That your brother—your half-brother, if you will—was an acquaintance of the man Braque."

Larne looked at him as if he were mad.

"An acquaintance of Braque!"

"You are surprised, but nevertheless it is true. There are witnesses who will say that they saw them talk together, as if they had an understanding."

Larne shook his head. "Well, if you can prove that, there's no more to say. But even if my brother was an associate of this man Braque, I am not responsible for the disreputable company he happened to keep."

"Nevertheless, we think it necessary that you should know," Gallois said patiently. "There are questions that must be asked of him, and you, perhaps, can tell us where he is."

"Questions?" An annoyance came over his face. "But you can't possibly imagine my brother had any tiling to do with the murder of Braque? I myself can prove that·" He broke off with a helpless wave of the hands. "Still, if you wish to question him, that is no affair of mine."

"M. Larne," began Gallois, as if laying down the position once and for all, "as a painter you are a very great man, but as what I am, I also am not without importance. In affairs of painting I accept your word, because there I am a nobody. In matters of law, you also accept my word. I say you are not responsible for your brother, and I do not say that your brother is the murderer of Braque, because that would be absurd. But there is information which your brother can perhaps give, and therefore I come to you to ask where it is I can find your brother."

Larne got to his feet.

"To-day I finished with my brother." His lip drooped. "Our relationships have not been either happy or—what shall I say?—advantageous. Where he is at this moment, I don't know. And, frankly, I don't care—provided he ceases to be an annoyance to me."

Gallois caught the subtle innuendo.

"M. Larne, I regret this interview, which appears to give you pain, and I assure you that when we have seen your brother there will be no more disturbance of yourself. But do you not know where it is possible that your brother should be?"

With an exaggerated patience, which still appeared to mask a considerable annoyance, Larne began to explain. Pierre had been living on him for years and he had got him out of no end of financial difficulties, so that the worry of him had become a very real hindrance to work. Then there was also the Villa. Hortense was a good soul, and her husband, when he was in health, helped to make a *ménage* that had its comforts. Then Bertrand fell ill and that took from the comfort, and altogether Larne had been going through a worrying time.

Then he decided to break with Pierre, and he admitted that he had paid him off. Hortense had wished to get away, and it had been arranged that she should go to a sister near Grenoble where the air might do Bertrand good. They had practically no private possessions, and Pierre had that morning taken them to Grenoble, and he had also taken his own few belongings. The car, which had been shared by the brothers, had been given to Pierre as part of the final settlement. Pierre had also been entrusted with a certain sum of money which a Grenoble bank would disburse as a small pension for Hortense. Larne, with a grimace which had its humour, admitted that at the moment he had left himself extremely short of funds. Not that he regretted it at all. For the first time for months, he felt himself an absolutely free man.

"That will excuse my apparent ill-humour," he said. "It was an unpleasant shock when you came here to begin these troubles with my brother all over again."

"Unhappily we do not yet commence to tell you about your brother," Gallois said. "But at this moment he will be perhaps, where?"

Larne shrugged his shoulders.

"He did not inform me of his intentions. Between ourselves, he was not in a very talkative mood when we parted. What I should imagine, though, is that he would spend the night somewhere near Dijon. Bertrand oughtn't to stand a longer journey than that."

"Sit down, I beg of you." The tone of Gallois had all at once a dry officialdom. "What I have with regret to tell you is that—"

"There's been an accident?"

Gallois smiled sadly.

"No accident has arrived. But when I am informed that your brother is an acquaintance of Braque, I at once have him under surveillance. An *agent* is dispatched to request that he sees me but this *agent* arrives to see him depart in a big car. He does not stop this car but he asks for instructions. How it arrives I am not permitted to inform you, but we find this car of your brother again. But it is not at Dijon. It is not in the direction of Grenoble that he travels at all! It is in the direction that is opposite! *It is near Fécamp that he is last seen.*"

Larne had been staring, mouth agape. His face flooded an angry red, and again he sprang to his feet. His hands were raised furiously to heaven, then he let out a deep breath and was sinking despairingly back in his chair.

"He deceives you, this Pierre," Gallois said apologetically.

"I was a fool," Larne said bitterly. "I ought to have known he'd be up to some trick." Then he was staring again at Gallois. "But why near Fécamp? What on earth should he be doing there?"

Gallois spread his hands.

"Perhaps this Hortense has a sister there also. Perhaps she arranges this with Pierre."

"It's inexplicable to me," Larne said. His face brightened. "Still, I accuse him of nothing. It will be for Hortense to make a complaint."

"It is also no affair of us," Gallois assured him. "That he deceives you is not a concern at all. But you understand, do you not, why M. Travers, who is your friend, insist that I convey to you the information."

He got to his feet, and his little bow had both courtesy and gratitude.

"Once more we apologize that we use your so valuable time, and we beg that you excuse us. And now we depart for Fécamp."

"But why?"

It was the turn of Gallois to look surprised.

"But it is still necessary that one should find your brother and question him about Braque. If he go to America, or China, or it matters not where, it is still necessary that he should be questioned."

"I suppose it is," Larne said slowly. "But there is a favour I would like to ask. I would like to confront him myself. If he has robbed me of money, then I have a hold over him. And there is still the question of Hortense."

"It is possible that we shall request that he returns with us to Paris," Gallois told him. In the same moment he had an idea. "But there is room in the car if you prefer to accompany M. Travers and myself."

Larne's face lighted for a moment, then fell.

"Unfortunately I couldn't. If you could wait for half an hour, perhaps?"

"But, why not?" Gallois told him. "It is necessary that we eat before we depart."

Larne shook his head fiercely.

"I can't eat till I know the truth. There's something behind all this."

"But we shall eat, and it is better perhaps that you eat also," Gallois said. "It is the truth that is often—what is the word?—uneatable."

"Unpalatable," suggested Travers. Gallois had seemed to refer to him, and be took it for a cue.

"I'm most distressed about all this," he said to Larne. "And I'm glad you're coming with us. Perhaps there'll be some perfectly simple explanation after all."

They came back to the hotel at the prearranged time, and found Larne waiting. At once the car moved off, Travers in front with the driver and Gallois at the back with Larne. In half an hour the outer suburbs were being passed, and at half-past eight they were through Pontoise and making for Gisors.

It was a dark night and blustery. The wind had shifted and was rising, and before morning, Gallois said, there would be rain. He and Larne talked little, and then not about that matter that was bringing them to Fécamp, so that Travers pricked his ears when there was a mention of Hortense.

Gallois had apparently asked for information about her. What with the noises of the car and the wind, Travers gathered little, except that it was Pierre who had engaged her through an agency, and it was always he who had arranged her and her husband's affairs, Larne himself being merely a kind of final judge in the matter of decisions or disputes.

But they were then in the outskirts of Rouen, and there the car stopped and Gallois disappeared for ten minutes. Of where he had been he said nothing, though he remarked that once they were through the city, half an hour's fast travelling would bring them to the journey's end. But they stopped first at Yvetot, where Gallois once more said he had a brief appointment, and when the car moved on again, it took the northerly road towards Sr. Valery.

Now they could smell the sea. The wind too was more blustery, and on the coast it would be a gale. At St. Valéry the car turned sharply left and every now and again (he sound of the breakers could be plainly heard. Then suddenly, in the middle of nowhere, Gallois had the car stopped, and he himself took the wheel.

To Travers it seemed that they were now on some side road. Now and again on the right the lights of the car revealed the melancholy sight of empty chalets and bathing-huts, and more than once in the distance could be seen the reflection of lights in the water and the faint glow that meant a town. On the left the ground rose in sandy dunes, with clumps of pines and small woods. Then suddenly the car was turning left and inland, and Gallois was driving at a mere crawl and peering ahead. Then he seemed to see the something for which he was looking, for he drew the car to a halt and switched off the lights. In the pitch-darkness that was all at once on them it was hard to see a hand before a face.

"We've arrived?" asked Travers.

Gallois, already getting out, announced that they had indeed arrived. A voice came startlingly from near by.

"*Qui est la?*"

Gallois whipped out a torch and flashed it. Travers discerned the figure of a man, and then Gallois was turning the torch on himself.

"*C'est moi—Gallois. Qu'est-ce qui est arrivé?*"

The man burst into a flood of explanations. He had been attacked, he said, and he was whipping off his cap and showing his head. Gallois moved forward into the dark and was apparently making an examination. The man began to talk again but Gallois checked him quickly.

"Remain there, gentlemen, if you please," he said. "In a minute I return."

He disappeared in the darkness with the man. Travers, hand on the car as if to retain his bearings, peered ahead and saw nothing. To what he judged was the west was the sound of the sea, but the lights of the town had gone, and he knew that the car was now behind the dunes. Then he stooped, and with eyes more accustomed to the dark, could see a kind of serrated blackness against the gloom of the sky. There was the scent of the pines and the soughing of the wind among the trees.

"Where on earth has Gallois brought us to?" Larne said peevishly.

But the flicker of a torch was seen ahead, and Gallois reappeared.

"Follow me, gentlemen," he said. "And remember always that it is I who ask the questions."

They followed close at his heels in the shifting sand, and then almost at once they were on a path. There was a hand-rail where the path mounted steeply, and then as Gallois once more flashed his torch, Travers could see that they were at the back of a tiny villa. The man who had hailed Gallois from the dark, was standing by. Gallois focused his light on the door, then knocked.

There was an echo from within the house, and in a minute Gallois knocked again, and stooped with his ear to the door. Then he shook his head, motioned for the man to remain where he was and beckoned for the two to follow. The force of the wind met them as they emerged through a gate to the side of the house, and once more in the distance Travers caught a glimpse of the lights of the town.

They came to the front door, with its path that seemed to lead down to the sea. Gallois flashed his torch again, and its light revealed the pink of the walls and the deep blue of the shutters and of the door. From inside the house there was never a crack of light.

Gallois knocked and listened.

"Remain here, if you please," he said again, and once more was moving off in the dark.

"What's happening?" whispered Travers to Larne. "Isn't your brother here after all?"

"Why should he be here?" Larne whispered fiercely. "This is like a nightmare. Why doesn't Gallois tell us what he's doing?"

His hand fell on Travers's arm.

"Did you hear that?"

Travers listened, breath held, and heard nothing but the swish of the trees and the soughing of the wind. The scent of the pines was very strong, and they seemed to be all about him.

Gallois reappeared. He had sent the man for the tool-bag of the car, he said, so that an entrance might be forced. When that tool-bag came, Travers held the torch and the man got to work on the fastening of a shutter. A pane was broken and the window hoisted. Another minute and he had opened the front door.

The light was on, and Gallois was telling the man to search downstairs. He himself made for the stairs at the end of the short passage, and soon his steps were heard in the rooms above. When he came down he was shaking his head, and nothing seemed more sure than that the house was deserted.

For a minute or two he walked restlessly from room to room, like a man who fails to see a clear way ahead, then all at once he made up his mind.

François was the name of the man, and Gallois was asking him if he had discovered who it was that had let the house. François spread his palms and regretted there had been time for nothing. He was going on with something else, but Gallois cut him short, and once more Travers had the feeling that there were things which Gallois was wishing to keep very much to himself.

"Go, then, and find out," he said. "The car will take you to the town and there is a telephone here by which you can report."

Then he was beckoning to Larne and Travers to follow him up the stairs. A bathroom and lavatory were there, and he pointed out the basin that had been used and the towel that was wet. Of the two bedrooms, one had a double bed, and the other had two single beds. All were made up ready for occupation, but one of the single beds was somewhat rumpled.

"They did come here?" Larne asked.

"But obviously," Gallois said.

"Then where are they?"

Gallois shrugged his shoulders.

"Perhaps they're coming back again," suggested Travers.

Gallois whipped open an empty drawer or two and made no comment.

"They've taken all their belongings?" asked the mystified Larne.

"Or else they did not unpack the belongings which they arrive with," Gallois said. "They arrive, and they eat, and then all at once they depart."

Then suddenly his hands sank and began to rise quiveringly to his shoulders. The repression of the last few minutes gave way to an extreme annoyance, but it was with himself that he was furious. English was inadequate, and from the French in which he upbraided himself, Travers gathered that he was an imbecile, the victim of an amazingly unfortunate chance, and that those who should have helped were *cretins* and incompetents.

Then he turned apologetically to Larne, and was himself again.

"It is for you that I am annoyed. I bring you all this way to see your brother, and he is not here. The fault, I assure you, is not all mine. But what can one do? For you to remain here is perhaps absurd. The car, then, is at your disposal, and it shall take you to Paris and your hotel."

Larne looked astounded.

"But why shouldn't my brother come back? Perhaps he changed his mind about Hortense and Bertrand and has taken them somewhere else."

Gallois shrugged his shoulders and began making his way out of the room. Downstairs it was icily cold, but he closed the shutter over the broken window, and turned on the little electric fire.

"Perhaps you will tell us more about this Hortense and this Bertrand," he said to Larne.

All Larne could do was to remind him once more that he knew nothing. Their name was Gurlot, and they had been engaged by Pierre and presented to himself as a kind of *fait accompli* when he arrived some years before at the Villa.

"And when is it that this Bertrand becomes ill?"

"About a year or more ago," Larne said. "But you must still understand that I have no time to enquire into the affairs of domestics. That is the business of Pierre. I was told by Pierre that Bertrand was ill and his lungs were giving him trouble. From time to time when I had to speak to Hortense, I asked how her husband was. It was only a few days ago that I was told he was really ill. I told Pierre he ought to go where he could be looked after." He thought for a moment. "That was it, and then the very next day after my arrival, Pierre mentioned the sister at Grenoble." He shrugged his shoulders. "I am not callous, but it seemed to me an excellent arrangement. Then there—"

He broke curiously off, with: "But that does not matter."

"You will pardon," said Gallois, "but there are times when everything matters. You were about to say?"

"Only this," Larne said. "There was a little private trouble which M. Travers here happened to witness, but I received the impression that my hand was being forced. My brother certainly knew that I was intending to get rid of him, and what I thought was that he and Hortense had schemed to get away as quickly as they could for some reasons of their own." His lip drooped. "I now appear to have been right, though what the reasons were, I still can't tell."

Gallois made no comment but he got to his feet.

"There is a garage here," he said. "Let us see if there is anything which we can learn."

The wind still seemed to be rising as they made their way to where their car had stood. A few yards back the light of the torch showed a cave-like garage made in the dune on the level of the road. Its door was closed but unlocked, and a look inside showed that it was made of stout boards roofed with more boards and tin. Gallois went methodically over the floor with his torch and apparently found nothing.

"A car *has* been in, and therefore out," he said, and showed the marks of tyres. "But there is also a boat-house which one must examine."

A lock had been hanging on the garage door, and when he had closed the place up, he put the key in his pocket. Then, as he moved off in the darkness to the right, the ground began to fall away, and they had to move sideways through the soft sand till they were on the bank of a tiny creek. A flash of the torch showed that the tide was receding.

But the torch showed no trace of footprints, and their own were already hidden by the shifting sand. Gallois shone the light ahead and there was the boathouse, its double doors opened and fastened back. A rowing-boat of medium size was moored there, but there was the space where another and larger boat had been.

"Remain here, if you please," Gallois said again, and made his way along the shelving bank. Then only his light was seen as he moved about inside the boat-house. For five good minutes he was there. Travers and Larne stood in the open with shoulders hunched against the wind, and the sting of the blown sand on their checks.

At last Gallois was coming back.

"There was a motor-boat," he said, "but it has gone. Now we return to the house."

The lights of the returning car were seen, but he ignored them and made his way up the same steep path to the house. The room struck warm after the chill of the wind. Gallois smiled mournfully at Larne as he drew a chair to the fire.

"There is no doubt, I think, that your brother has departed? But it is a strange departure. Not only does one go by car, one also leaves by boat, and that to me is inexplicable."

"It is to me," Larne said. "It's a nightmare. Either I'm mad or—well, the whole world's mad."

Gallois nodded as if in agreement, then made for the phone. The receiver went to his car, then he was looking puzzled. Then he was pulling the flex which came up in his hand.

Back went the receiver and he was making a gesture as if it was the phone he wanted to upbraid.

"Now I think you agree that your brother does not return?" he said to Larne. "One does not cut the telephone when one merely absents one's self for a time."

He glared at the phone again, then picked up the end of cut flex. He looked at it under his glass, and Travers came across and looked at it too.

"It is some hours that it has been cut," Gallois said. "There is a film of damp which makes a commencement of rust."

Then before Travers could get a close view he was angrily letting the flex fall.

"All the same," he announced, "there is an agreement. It is now ten o'clock, and it was at five o'clock, as I calculate, that they arrive here. It is at five o'clock that one informs me that one has seen the car, which makes apparently for Fécamp. They arrive but they do not unpack, as we agree, and at once they depart. I say 'at once' because it is some hours since the wire was cut, and one does not cut the wire till one is in the act of departing."

Larne was looking bewildered.

"But they left at eight o'clock this morning! They must have been here long before five o'clock?"

"They wish to conceal their tracks," Gallois explained. "They make detours and they do not arrive here till it is almost dark. But of the arrival I am certain, and of the departure." Once more his hands rose annoyedly. "Even while I am at your hotel to announce that your brother is here, he is not here. He has already gone."

"But why *should* he go?" asked Travers.

"Because he became aware that he was being observed," Gallois said. "He observed during the day that he was followed, and that was why he made the detours and why he succeeds that we lose the car. Then he arrives here and he thinks he is safe, but he observes that imbecile of a François, and he knows he is not safe. In the dusk he surprises this François and knocks him on the head. Then he cuts the phone and he departs, in order that he may be safe at some other place."

Suddenly he was turning on Larne.

"This Bertrand Gurlot, he can drive a car?"

"Not to my knowledge," Larne said. "But nothing I think I know turns out to be right."

"Perhaps, then, he drives the car and departs with his wife, and Pierre gives them money. Not all the money, but enough that will satisfy. Then Pierre takes the motor-boat himself."

"Yes, but why? Why should he run away like this?"

"There is something which commences to be serious," Gallois said, "unless your brother thinks that it is *you* who arrange to follow him, and that it is you who put François to watch. If that is so, then it is once more no affair of mine. Your brother deceives you, and he thinks you have discovered this deception and that he robs you, and so he escapes. That, I repeat, is no affair of mine. Nevertheless, I wish to find your brother in order that he may tell us what he knows of this Braque, of whom he is an associate."

Larne was about to speak, but Gallois waved a hand.

"That is one thing," he said, "but there is also the other. If it is not from *you* that your brother escapes, then he escapes because of *me*. Not of me, Gallois, but of the law. That is why the affair acquires a seriousness, and why it is of a necessity that we should find your brother."

Larne shook his head.

"I still refuse to believe that Pierre had anything to do with the murder of Braque. I can prove that he was elsewhere at the time—"

Gallois broke wearily in. "M. Larne, no one accuses your brother of such a crime. Nevertheless, there may be complicities of which you are not aware. And there remains the fact that it is in a panic that your brother has left this house, and has separated himself from the Gurlots. And since what we discover may be of pain to yourself, return to Paris in the car, I beg of you, and leave us here to our examination. In the morning, I assure you, I will do myself the honour of informing you if there is anything we discover that concerns yourself."

Larne shook his head determinedly.

"I've come all this way and I'm not going back till I know more. This is driving me crazy, and I've *got* to find something out."

It was to Travers that he had spoken, and Travers had a suggestion to make.

"Stay at a hotel here—at Fécamp, I mean. There's no need to worry yourself like this. You're not responsible for your brother." Then he had an idea. "I shouldn't be surprised if you find the two Gurlots waiting for you at the hotel to-morrow morning with the car, and asking to be allowed to go back to the Villa. So you go to the town and get a meal and a good night's rest."

Larne shook his head, then thought again and got to his feet. "Perhaps you're right. I think I will go after all. There's nothing I can do here?"

"If you will have the goodness to answer one or two questions," Gallois said hastily. "You suspect for some time, do you not, something that is secret between Hortense Gurlot and your brother?"

Larne cast a quick look at Travers.

"I've already told you I've suspected it."

"It is possible that this Hortense is—or was—the mistress of your brother?"

Larne's lip curled. "It is possible. But my brother was not a king of France. He should have had a better taste in mistresses."

"For myself, I have not the time for affairs of the sort," Gallois told him, "and therefore it is not with authority that I speak. But this money that you give your brother this morning or last night—"

"Last night."

Gallois nodded. "Your brother also had money before you pay him that sum?"

Larne's lip curled again. "He told me he hadn't a sou. That may have been to get more out of me."

"Then that is all," announced Gallois. "at Fécamp you will arrange a hotel, and in the morning I will do myself the honour of telling you what there is that we discover. But of that, I hope nothing. When everyone has disappeared, there is no one to interrogate."

He ushered Larne out and Travers went with them to the car. A gust of wind met them at the turn, and almost drove them back on their feet. Gallois halted.

"At dusk, when one departs in the motor-boat, the sea is calm," he said. "Now it is impossible that so small a boat should exist. It is with regret that I say it, but there is something, M. Larne, which one must not disregard."

Larne shook his head but said nothing. At the car Gallois uttered the most profuse of thanks, and added that he was a fool to have mentioned the danger of the sea. Perhaps Pierre had observed that for himself, and had already put in somewhere to land.

The car moved off and its rear light disappeared round the bend. The voice of Gallois had at once a new alertness.

"And now, my friend, to work. There are other things it is necessary to explain."

CHAPTER XII
END OF AN EPISODE

GALLOIS DREW IN HIS CHAIR again to the fire. There were things to consider, he said, before they made another examination of the rooms. Then he was smiling at Travers in a curious, apologetic kind of way.

"Did I not tell you, my friend, that you would be annoyed with me before everything was finished."

"Well, I'm not annoyed yet," Travers told him. "But why did you remind me of that?"

"Because there are lies which I am forced to tell," Gallois said. "It is necessary that I deceive you, because it is necessary that I also deceive M. Larne. At the moment I do not wish him to know the truth. If you demand why, I tell you this. There are things which he knows, as you also are aware, and in order that he may tell us these things, it is necessary to act with finesse,"

"He's certainly told you more to-night than he's ever done before," Travers said, and still failed to see the point. "But just what were the lies you told?"

"I did not know that Pierre and the Gurlots had arrived at Fécamp," Gallois said calmly. "When the car makes this way for the coast, and is lost, then I imagine that it makes for some port of embarkation, and one watches the roads towards Le Havre and Boulogne. Then just before I arrive at your hotel I hear that a car such as we seek is seen at Yvetot, where a woman purchased goods in the shops, but this car is gone again before one can make sure. I say to myself that there are three ways which it may go, and I guess that it is Fécamp."

"Good lord!" said Travers. "Do you mean to say you brought Larne all the way here when his brother mightn't have been here at all?"

"Ah, but I stop at Rouen to enquire if there is more news, and I learn that I am right. Later I stop again, and I find the name of the house and that François watches."

"That was a lucky hit of yours," Travers said. "And was that all the lies you told?"

"No," said Gallois. "François arrived to find the house dark, and he saw also the garage which was closed." He shook his head. "He is an imbecile, that one. He shows his torch everywhere so that all the world can observe, but he does not show it inside the garage and remark the car has gone, or that it has not gone. It is about half-past eight, and there is always no light from the house, and then suddenly he is struck on the head, and when he awakes, he is tied at the arms and feet. But he disengages himself, and it is soon after then that we arrive."

"But if there was no one in the house, who struck him on the head and tied him up?"

"That we do not know," Gallois admitted. "But what I say is this. Before François arrived, either the car or the motor-boat had already gone. But as it was necessary for the party to divide themselves, one of them returned. But he could not take the car or the boat because of François, who would have heard. So he waits an occasion and hits this François on the head, and while he is unconscious, he departs with the car or the boat."

Travers had only half heard, for he had been doing some quick thinking of his own. He was filling to see, for instance, how those particular lies and concealments would help to loosen Larne's tongue and make him reveal all he knew or suspected about Pierre. Yet Larne certainly did know a good deal. He had confessed as much by hints and signs that morning at the Villa when there had been that queer scene with Pierre and Hortense.

"You still do not understand?" Gallois was saying.

"Yes," prevaricated Travers. "I think perhaps I do."

"Then we will go upstairs," Gallois said, and at once led the way.

He made for the room with two beds, and examined again the one that was rumpled.

"It is your opinion that someone has been upon this bed?" he asked Travers.

"I'd say there's no doubt about it," Travers told him. "There's the depression on the pillow where the head was."

"Then who was it that was on the bed?"

"Bertrand," said Travers promptly. "He needn't have been, as ill as was made out to Larne, but he was tired after the long journey, and he lay on this bed and rested."

"That is also my opinion."

At once he was going down the stairs again, and now he made for the kitchen. The plates on the dresser were examined and the contents of the drawers, and at last he and Travers were agreed that two people only had eaten and drunk, while the third—Bertrand—rested upstairs.

"We arrive then at what one calls the end of an episode," Gallois announced. "It remains to reassemble the pieces and make them into one. But first, a question. Is it your opinion that Pierre was the assassin of Braque?"

Travers shook his head. "I don't think he was. Although his brother won't tell you the details, I believe he can prove that Pierre was at the Villa at the time."

"Then who remains?" Gallois asked himself. "There is Cointeau, perhaps. That client who establishes his alibi does not yet arrive. There is the woman Moulins, but she has an alibi which is more than perfect. And who else is there?"

A peculiar look accompanied the question, as if he awaited the answer only in order to refute it or to give some answer of his own.

"There *is* no one else," Travers said. "Those are the only people with whom we've come into contact."

"Ah," said Gallois, and raised a dramatic finger. "There is yet another. *There is this Bertrand, whom we have never seen!*"

Travers stared, then all at once, was polishing his glasses.

"You're right. As you say, there's this Bertrand, whom neither you nor I have ever seen. We don't know just how ill he was. All that tale to Henri Larne might have been a carefully thought out plot. It almost certainly was."

"Then we arrive at this," Gallois said. "The Gurlots and Pierre were associates of Braque. Pierre knew that the patience of his brother would be soon exhausted, and he decides that he will make money from this gold-mine of which Braque is the owner. From Braque he discovers everything, and then he makes his plans. I suspect that this house was arranged, and the murder was then arranged also. While Pierre has his alibi, Bertrand does the murder and takes also the money with which to work the gold-mine. If anything is discovered about Bertrand, then Pierre and Hortense swear to an alibi for him also. Then they arrange that Bertrand shall be very ill and M. Larne agrees that he goes away. Pierre profits from the occasion to obtain more money from his brother, and this morning they all depart.

"But all the time they have what you call the guilty conscience. They observe that they are followed but they contrive to lose the man who follows. Then they quarrel and say it is dangerous to go to Fécamp. Then at last they must go somewhere, and they agree to arrive here when it is dusk. But they will stay only a short time perhaps, and then they agree that Bertrand shall depart with Hortense in the car—"

Then suddenly he broke off. His lean fingers clawed the air and in a moment he had the solution he sought.

"But, no. All that I have said is wrong. We commence once more at the beginning and this is what arrives. Bertrand comes to the bedroom to regard from the window if there is still anyone who has followed, and when he is not watching he rests on the bed. But soon be has a suspicion. Then the light from the torch of François reveals that there is someone who watches. Imagine to yourself, my friend, what happens here in this house. There are no lights and they watch this torch of François and they expect every minute that the police will arrive. It is necessary that they make an escape but it is impossible. Then Pierre has his idea. It is he who surprises François, and then it is possible that they all escape. It is Pierre, I think, who takes the motor-boat, and it is the Gurlots who take the car."

"And where are they now?"

Gallois shrugged his shoulders.

"This Pierre, I do not think he is drowned, I think he arranges a rendezvous in Belgium, perhaps, and he makes his way along the coast. The car it takes the third-class roads, and it also arrives at the rendezvous."

"Then it may take days before you lay your hands on them!" said the stupefied Travers.

"Arrest them, you would say?" He smiled sadly. "At the moment it is not our affair if they go to Belgium. That is not a crime. It would be wise, perhaps, that we should discover where it is that they hide themselves, but there is something of an importance still greater that we must do."

He leaned across to pat Travers on the arm.

"You and I, my friend, we make some theories that are excellent, but it remains that these theories should be changed to facts. We have yet to prove that these people commit a crime. It is to Paris therefore that we return."

"To-night?"

"In the morning," Gallois said. "Soon one may discover this Pierre and these Gurlots, and they will be interrogated." He smiled with something of amusement. "If there are questions which one can have the ingenuity to find. But doubtless already they have for us a story that is of the most plausible, and once more we arrive at nothing. Therefore in the morning we go to Paris. There, perhaps, we discover what is this gold-mine of the dead Braque, and what it is that M. Larne suspects about his brother. Out of that will arise perhaps some questions to which this Pierre and these Gurlots have not already arranged the answers."

"And in the meanwhile, what?"

Gallois got to his feet.

"Now we go to find the owner of this house. With that you agree?"

Travers was only too pleased. For one thing, he was thinking to himself as they made their way down to the car, he would at least hear something at first hand. Before Francois had hardly opened his mouth, Gallois had hurried him away, and had later related his own version of the attack. All the time, in fact, Travers had had that feeling that Gallois was holding back evidence, or arranging it to suit some extraordinary private end. All that night the Inspector had been like two men: one who is in a hopeless fog, and another who is gifted with second sight, plus the most uncanny luck.

At the car Gallois had a word with the driver and then announced that the owner of the house had been found. He was a M. Archon of Fécamp, and he proposed to interview him at once.

It was a short, stout man who opened the door.

"M. Archon?" said Gallois.

"Yes, and you are M. Gallois?" he said, and at once was showing the two in. Gallois was producing his credentials, but Archon insisted that it was unnecessary.

"Everyone knows the famous Inspector Gallois," he said. "We are provincial here, but we read our papers."

The gratified Gallois introduced Travers, who, he said, spoke an excellent French, but who needed a slowness and a carefulness in order to follow it well.

Archon showed them into an old-fashioned parlour of a room that was stuffy with the heat from a monstrous stove, He was a chatty soul, full of self-possession and quite a likeable importance. He insisted that they should drink, and produced a very fine cognac.

"It is this *affaire* Braque that brings you to Fécamp?" he suggested to Gallois.

"The *affaire* Braque?" One would have thought he had never heard of it. Then he was making a gesture of indifference. "But there are other *affaires* than that of this Braque. At the moment we occupy ourselves with a gang of swindlers."

Archon stared.

"Yes," said Gallois. "A gang of swindlers who arranged, one assumes, to operate from your house."

"He was a swindler, that M. Foulange!"

"So he called himself Foulange," said Gallois. "Tell us, if you please, everything you know, and above all about this M. Foulange."

Archon said that the previous Sunday a M. Foulange had called to see him. He had evidently inspected the house on the dunes and had taken a fancy to it. Provided it was made ready for immediate occupation, he would hire it for three months, with an option of renewal, and he would pay in advance. Archon was only too ready to agree. That house was usually let in the season only, and rarely before May, so he was that much money to the good. Foulange paid down a small deposit, and it was arranged that the beds should be aired and everything ready by the Wednesday.

"Describe to me this M. Foulange," Gallois said.

The description fitted Pierre Larne to the life, so Travers privately hinted.

"And he arrived on the Wednesday?" Gallois said.

"But, no," Archon told him. "it was not till the Thursday afternoon that he arrived, which is yesterday. Together we inspected the house and he was very satisfied. Then here in this house he paid me the three months' rent in advance. You would wish to see the agreement?"

"Not at the moment," Gallois said. "But how did he pay you? In cash?"

"In cash," echoed Archon. "He had to me the air of a rich man. From his pocket he produced a bundle of notes, as big as this."

Once more Gallois and Travers exchanged glances.

"And what reasons did he give you for coming here?" Gallois asked.

"It is not my business to question clients," Archon said with dignity. "But of his own accord he told me this. He had a brother who was ill and to whom the doctors had ordered the sea air. He also had a housekeeper. For himself he said he was a writer, and a bit of a recluse. He also was fond of fishing, which was why he was so gratified at the excellent condition of the motor-boat. He said he would use it for fishing, and I should charge a supplementary let. Generally he would use the rowing-boat, which was free, or the dinghy."

"What dinghy?" asked Gallois.

"The dinghy attached to the motor-boat," Archon explained. "It is a big motor-boat that will, if necessary, accommodate four or five."

There was some technical talk which Travers could not altogether gather, but Gallois explained that the boat was turtle-decked and was really a tiny converted yacht. When Archon said it would hold four or five, he was not meaning that they could sleep in it, but could sail in it. There was the most cramped cabin accommodation for one only.

"One could cross the Channel with such a boat?" asked Travers.

"To England? But certainly," he said. "Naturally it depends on the weather."

His consternation was considerable when Gallois told him the boat and dinghy were missing, and on such a night. They might be recovered, of course, but that particular affair was one for the local police, to whom Archon must make his complaint. Then, with many thanks, Gallois was rising to go.

"Though you have for the moment lost your boat," he told Archon consolingly, "you have at least the money of this Foulange in your pocket. And now, M. Archon, good night and good sleep. It is possible that in a day or two I may see you again. In the meantime, if there is anything that you remember, communicate it to me direct."

"And where now?" asked Travers, as Gallois made for the car again.

"Back to the house," Gallois said. "There are doubtless finger-prints which I must take, and later I must return here to telephone. You, my friend, shall provide yourself with blankets from upstairs and rest before the fire. If I am absent, there is that imbecile of a François who remains on guard."

As for the evidence that Archon had just provided, it seemed, as he said, overwhelmingly in support of those theories at which he and Travers had arrived. The murder had been planned in conjunction with the hiring of the house, and most damning had been the disclosure that Foulange had not paid till after the murder of Braque. Then he had been able to flourish under the eyes of Archon perhaps the very wad of notes that Braque had waved beneath the nose of Cointeau.

It had rained in the night, but the morning dawned cold and grey, and it was a silent and thoughtful party who returned to Paris in the car. On the way there were no halts, and the car did not stop till Larne was being set down at his hotel.

Gallois must have had some private talk with him, so Travers gathered from the last words that were said.

"I regret to acknowledge it, but you have convinced me that Pierre is deeply involved," he told Gallois. "All the same, you must eliminate from your mind any idea that he was concerned in the murder. As for me, I now wash my hands of him. He has dishonoured a name, and all I can most humbly request is that there should be no publicity. I owe that much to myself."

Gallois drew himself up with a dignity.

"You forget, M. Larne, that I also have the soul of a poet. Your name is not only your own; it is the honoured possession of all France. Nothing to the detriment of that name, I assure you, shall ever emerge."

The two clasped hands, and then Larne was sadly shaking his head.

"My mind is made up. In two days or three, as soon as I can arrange my affairs, I sail for America. There is an aunt, and an uncle, I have not seen for years—the sister and brother of my mother. But I shall naturally communicate to you an address."

"You are right," Gallois told him with conviction. "It is annoyances like these that prevent work and clog the brain. In the meanwhile, a thousand thanks, and an infinity of regrets."

Bernice had been warned by phone that Travers was arriving at about ten o'clock. It was still short of that hour, and Gallois had a few words with Travers in the lobby of the hotel. The case seemed as good as over, he admitted. Nothing remained to do but to lay hands on all or even one of the three, and submit them to a severe interrogation. The matter of the loss of the motor-boat would be a pretext.

"So there's nothing more for me to do?" asked Travers.

Gallois frowned. "There is this matter of Charles, who pretends to be your valet—an idea which doubtless seems to you to have at times an air of the ridiculous. But it is necessary that he should convince the woman Moulins. Pierre, or the Gurlots, may return to Paris, where it is the most easy to conceal one's self and where perhaps they have friends. The woman Moulins may possibly remember some other associate of Braque, who is their friend, and thus one arrives at an arrest."

He was smiling sympathetically as he held out his hand.

"You are dispirited, my friend, but all I say is— patience and always patience; for what you have done there is nothing to say, because we are friends. To-day you will rest. To-morrow, perhaps, there will be other news. Meanwhile continue, I ask you, your co-operation in the matter of this Moulins. It is necessary that Charles devours her thoughts as one devours the flesh of an orange. And after that—"

A shrug of the shoulders conveyed the rest, but it left a curious foreboding in Travers's mind. As for the background of disappointment which had given such a dispirited look to his face, Bernice took it for tiredness. She had been very worried about him, she said, and was glad he was having little more to do with the wretched business.

"I don't think widowhood agrees with me," she told him. "This afternoon you shall rest, and then if you feel like it, we can go to a cinema and dine out. That will brighten you up. And we'll think of something really nice to do to-morrow."

But Travers's rest was disturbed soon after lunch. Charles arrived with a request. Would it be possible for him to drive Travers somewhere in the car so that the two could be observed by Elise?

Travers told him the arrangements that had been made for the evening, and added that he was damned if he would alter them, or turn out that afternoon, for anyone short of the President of the Republic.

Charles grinned. The evening's arrangements would suit him to perfection, he said. He would drive the car and might even arrange that he and Elise should go to the same cinema.

"And how do you continue to find her—this Elise?" Travers asked ironically.

"One cannot tell," said Charles, and his face took on a seriousness. "In these affairs it is necessary to act with patience and finesse."

"I seem to have heard that somewhere before," Travers remarked with a certain dryness. "But in herself, how do you find her?"

Charles lost all his glibness and was stammering this and that. Travers gathered that one might have been deceived, that she had a good heart, and that there are those whose misfortunes are not their faults. And so much for Charles.

That night Travers returned, as he assured himself, for the very last time to a consideration of the case, and soon he was once more realizing the one thing. If the case was as good as over, and the theories of Gallois and himself were correct, then he himself was hopelessly disappointed.

That led him as usual to a search for flaws that might demolish the theories that only a few hours before had seemed so foolproof, and, indeed, attractive. But all he could find were certain things that puzzled him.

In the first place, if Pierre had stolen some of those studies of his brother, or even a finished picture, how could Braque have disposed of them? It would not have been like selling the work of a dead painter. However plausible the tongue of Braque, and however fanatical the buyer, and indifferent as to how he acquired possession of a Larne, yet the fact remained that Braque would be running too colossal a risk. The buyer would be bound to suspect some swindle, and it would be to the painter—the living painter—that he would apply, however surreptitiously, for information. Then the whole swindle would become public.

Then there was that attempt that had been made on the life of Larne, and how he had hushed it up. Was it Pierre who had tried to kill his brother in the south of France? And if so, what connection was there with the killing of Braque? Had Larne discovered something, and was that attempt on his life also a hint that he had better keep his eyes shut and his mouth closed?

And lastly, Travers had discovered another lie that Gallois had perpetrated and had not confessed. He had said that it was only at Rouen—the time then being about a quarter-past eight—that he knew the house where Pierre and the Gurlots were occupying. Yet Gallois had also said before, that the party had come to the house and then had cut the telephone wire and bolted soon after dusk. In other words, two hours after the party had come and gone, Gallois had discovered they were arriving. Involved, perhaps, but not nearly so involved as the whole story of Gallois and the explanations he had dished out from time to time about Fécamp, and the house, and all those nightmare experiences of the previous night.

And then Travers had to smile to himself. There he was, being annoyed with Gallois, just as Gallois himself had prophesied. Something uncanny about that foresight of Gallois, and then Travels was remembering something else: the grimness and even the callousness with which Gallois had mentioned that devouring the very thoughts of Elise Moulins as one devours the pulp of an orange and throws away the skin. Yes, thought Travers, and shook his head, there was also about Gallois a something that was frightening, and he could tell himself that in some ways he was glad he was having little more to do with the case.

CHAPTER XIII
THE AMAZING NIGHT

THE MORNING WAS fine and cold, the kind of morning, in fact, to make the blood run cheerfully through the veins. Travers felt himself again, and after breakfast he could once more turn his thoughts to the case.

But not for long. When, for instance, he tried to work out all those movements of Pierre at Fécamp, and fit the times in, and make all coincide with those voluble explanations that had been given by Gallois, he could achieve nothing but the most amazing muddle. If one took those explanations for gospel, then Pierre and the Gurlots were in the house when they should have been out, and most certainly out when they should have been in, and altogether when Travers reviewed things in the cold light of that February morning, there was such a hotch-potch of conflicting times and movements that would have done no disgrace to a first-class nightmare.

As for Gallois, Travers could not help but feel that he had been behaving with such finesse that he had come very near to being ridiculous. A hard thing to think but Travers was forced to it. The art of successful co-operation was surely a perfect confidence. Gallois, who had been the first to insist on the merits, and to prophesy the success, of the co-operation, was apparently disposed to regard the mystifying of his partner as the first essential, and to excuse it by ambiguous hints about deceiving Henri Larne was only to add chicanery to obscurity.

Not that Travers was in the least annoyed. He was rather disposed to put some blame on himself, and a failure to get clean under the hide of one who was so eccentric in his methods as Gallois. And in good time, he presumed, he would at least be vouchsafed by Gallois some real and comprehensible reason for the eccentricities. Meanwhile it was a fine morning, and the case could rest in Gallois' own hands, so the Traverses took a taxi to the Bois, and walked and lunched there, and it was not till two o'clock that they returned to the hotel.

Bernice then had an engagement, but Travers was content to spend the afternoon before the fire with a book. Just when he was wondering if he should have an early tea, Charles appeared. He had come, it appeared, merely to kill time or to satisfy his conscience.

"Nothing new has happened?" Travers asked him.

"Nothing," Charles said. "One has examined the finger-prints on the articles that M. Gallois brings back from Fécamp, but they tell us nothing."

"Apparently everything now depends on you," Travers told him amusedly. "Which reminds me. Was your friend Elise properly impressed at the sight of me yesterday evening?"

"She thinks that you have a face that is very kind," Charles said. "She agrees with me that you have a good heart. She says also that you have an air of much intelligence, like a professor, but I do not agree. It is necessary that she should think you are rich, and perhaps kind, but not that you are clever."

Travers laughed. "So long as you insist that I'm also virtuous, I don't mind about the rest. You, I take it, are still occupying the kitchen?"

Charles looked the least bit self-conscious.

"Now I am employed, I obtain very soon a room that is nearer than Belleville."

Travers smiled bewilderedly. "I still can't quite make out why you're going to all this trouble to convince that girl that you're what you are not."

Charles seemed rather hurt at that, and he smiled with a sad reproof that gave him once more that extraordinary resemblance to Gallois.

"You have read *Monsieur Lecoq*? You remember the pretended Mai, and that for months, even when he was unobserved, he was indeed the artist of the circus that he claimed to be?"

"I remember it well," admitted Travers. "But books and real life are no comparisons."

Charles gave that attractive smile of his own.

"You remember then, monsieur, a certain poor but honest man who asked help of you in the rue Jourdoise, and how even the driver of the taxi was deceived?"

"Yes," said Travers, "You've got me there. But has she told you anything else about Braque?"

"It is a subject which is painful," Charles said. "Naturally she does not wish to recall episodes which may be distasteful to me also." He shook his head, then went on almost defiantly. "In these affairs one must proceed with—"

"With patience and finesse," interrupted Travers. "It is a phrase with which I am becoming well acquainted. But, as I was asking, you are learning nothing at all?"

"I hear all about her family but never about Braque. He is something of which she does not wish to be reminded. Even that picture—you know about the picture?"

"You mean the one she offered to sell Braque? The one, you might say, that first made them acquainted?"

"That is the picture, and now it reminds her of Braque and she wishes again to sell it. I say that it is wrong to sell the only thing one has belonging to an only brother."

"What sort of a picture is it?" Travers asked.

Charles grimaced. "As monsieur already knows, I am ignorant about pictures. This one is the head of a man. It is perhaps expressive, but—"

"In other words, you don't care a lot about it." Then he was frowning. "That old professor we saw, he had a very high opinion of her brother's work, but, of course, you weren't able to tell her that." He frowned to himself again. "I don't know that I wouldn't like to have a look at that picture myself. If she really wants to sell it, and I like it—"

Charles was getting excitedly to his feet.

"But why not see the picture? I will arrange."

"Gently, gently," said Travers. "I'm not going to have you commit me to anything in order that you may ingratiate yourself with this Elise. All you're at liberty to say is that you knew I was a collector of pictures and so you mentioned her picture to me. Then I said you might bring it for my inspection."

Charles shook his head.

"But, monsieur, she would not do things like that. It is better that you present yourself at her apartment. It is I who will arrange everything."

"You will accompany me?"

"But certainly."

Travers shook his head. "But I still don't want to go to her apartment."

Charles spread his hands imploringly.

"But, monsieur, this is an opportunity that will never again present itself. I assure you it is perfectly natural that you go with me to the apartment. She will think—"

"Very well," cut in Travers, and grimaced. "Get it arranged when I'm to come, and let me know."

Charles departed like a schoolboy going to a treat. Travers had merely in the back of his mind the idea that in a day or two, maybe, Charles would suggest a suitable time for the proposed visit, and the wind was taken clean out of his sails when he appeared again that same evening, just after dinner. Travers gave a somewhat sketchy explanation to Bernice, and was only too conscious of the fact that Elise had been the least bit over-emphasized.

"I never did quite understand that joke about Charles," Bernice said frowningly. "And, darling, why do you want to buy the picture?"

"I don't," protested Travers. "All the same, I'm always ready to pick up a bargain."

"You're sure it isn't some horrible plot!" said the suddenly alarmed Bernice. "There was that other dreadful affair when you went to see that man Braque."

Travers assured her that the visit was as safe, and the locality as public, as Bond Street.

It was a fine night and Charles said it might look strange if he drove the car in mufti as he was, and it was also not worth the trouble of a taxi. Almost at once he was turning into a side street along which they proceeded for a good half-mile. Then he was moving off to the right again, through an ill-lighted passage, then into a narrow, gloomy street, and so through a passage again to what looked like a dark cul-de-sac. Travers was leaving the cobbled road for the greater comfort of the narrow pavement, when Charles announced that they had arrived.

"Not a very salubrious district?" whispered Travers.

Charles's shrug of the shoulders seemed to ask what was it that Travers had expected. Then he was pushing open a door and turning on the light. Travers saw ahead a steep flight of dirty-looking stairs, and when he had come to the landing above them, Charles switched off the light and switched on another. They mounted more stairs, and it was when they were almost at the top that a slit of light suddenly appeared, as if a door had partly opened.

"C'est toi, Charles?"

"Oui, c'est moi—et monsieur le patron."

The door opened and a light flooded the top landing. As Elise drew back to let the two men pass, Travers had a good view of her. There seemed a vast difference from when he had first seen her in Larne's studio that night. All that assurance, that air of petulance and bravado which, according to Charles, had been her armour of defence, had certainly gone, and had left merely a woman, but a decidedly attractive one at that.

"Enter, monsieur," she said to Travers. "I am very grateful that you should come."

"It is I who am grateful," he told her, eyes already searching the walls. It was a look which she misinterpreted.

"One is not too comfortable here," she said apologetically. "But when one has not too much money, one lives where one can."

"But to me it has the air of being very comfortable," protested Travers. "It is a room that does you credit."

She seemed pleased at that, though she shook her head.

"I did not wish that you should trouble yourself, but it was M. Charles who assured me that you would wish to come yourself."

Charles cut in hastily with the indication of a chair on which Travers must sit, and he took up his position behind it rather like a footman at the elbow of some important diner.

"And this is the picture of which you wish to dispose?" asked Travers, craning his neck to look at it.

"That is the picture," she said. "It was given by my brother who also painted it. At the time I was only a girl."

Travers swivelled round in his chair, polished his glasses and looked at it from where he sat, which was within about six feet. It was an oil, some eighteen inches by twelve; the head of a man, as Charles had said, and in a style that recalled Van Gogh. But it was a hasty bit of work, and in many ways curious. It looked like a portrait of a not too interesting subject, and Travers was feeling in all sorts of minds about it. He could discern a merit, and the picture in some ways attracted him, and yet he was aware that his knowledge was scarcely equal to a real judgment of the picture's value, even within the scope of the exceedingly modest price he was likely to be asked.

There was much more he would like to know about it, he thought, and then was realizing that there were things perhaps that she would not care to discuss in the presence of Charles. There was a certain restraint already that he could feel in the room, and it went beyond a mere respect for his own silence.

"Your brother had certainly a talent," he pronounced.

Then he was feeling in his pocket and making a gesture of annoyance.

"I have no cigarettes. Go along at once, Charles, and buy some."

"Monsieur will pardon, but I myself have—"

"They are not those that I prefer," Travers told him curtly. "And hurry, please. One cannot waste the time of mademoiselle all night."

The door closed on Charles, and he smiled friendlily at the watchful Elise.

"There are things perhaps which one does not wish all the world to know. This picture that your brother painted, why was it that it was not purchased by a dealer of the knowledge of M. Braque?"

Her cheeks coloured, but she made no hesitation about telling him.

"But he did wish the picture." She shook her head as if wondering how to make herself clear. "I offer it to him and he says perhaps he can sell. Then he brings it back and says he one day may have a client. Then later he comes here and says he changes his mind and he will buy the picture. But I am angry and I also do not then wish the money, and I do not sell. He begs of me but I do not sell. Then he changes his mind and he says he does not wish the picture, and he makes me promise if I will sell, it will be to him."

Her checks flushed again.

"Then after we quarrel he comes here and I refuse to let him enter. I say it is all finished and I will never see him again, and that if he is an annoyance, I will tell the police. Then he pretends not to be angry and he asks only if I will sell the picture. I refuse and he says it does not matter. Then he goes away and I do not see him again. But I think perhaps that he will try and steal the picture, and I hide it. Then when he is dead, I hang it again there."

Travers nodded, but inwardly he was extraordinarily puzzled.

"It sounds to me as if he couldn't make up his mind whether the picture was worth anything or not. And you yourself have had it for a long time?"

Then she began telling him about her brother, and how she thought that during his last few years in France he had managed to exist by painting portraits, like the one on the wall. Most of the money had gone on drink, and when he disappeared she could only think he was dead. It was quite a shock when she heard five years ago that he had died in Algiers. Some time she was hoping to go there and learn more, but unhappily she had lost the letter that the priest had sent.

Then she was listening, for there was the sound of feet on the stairs. But there was the sound of voices also, and one of them was the angry voice of Charles. Then the feet began to mount, the arguing voices still going on. Elise had got frightenedly to her feet.

"What is happening?"

"It is nothing," Travers said, but he was already at the door. But he opened it only for Charles to enter, and with him, holding his arm, was a burly man whom Travers had never seen. Far down the stairs other voices could still be heard.

"What is it?" demanded Travers.

The two began to talk at once. Then Charles got in ahead. He was returning with the cigarettes, he said, when he was stopped by the police and asked where he was going. He explained all, and then was requested to return in the company of the *agent.*

The *agent,* who had listened stolidly enough, was producing his credentials, and handing them to Elise.

"Sit down," he said curtly to Charles. "And you also, monsieur." His hand went out for the credentials again. "You are Elise Moulins, known as Deschamps?"

Her whole expression had changed. There was the hard look again, and a defiance that had also a touch of despair.

"Yes, but there is nothing that I have done."

The *agent* shrugged his shoulders. "That is not my concern. You will accompany me, if you please." He looked round at the two men. "My instructions were to bring also everyone who was here. Your name is?"

"Rabaud—Charles Rabaud."

That the *agent* was a party to the comedy, Travers was well aware, but the name was written down.

"Occupation?"

"I am the chauffeur of this gentleman. But I also protest. There is nothing—"

"Un peu de silence!" the agent told him curtly. "And you, monsieur?"

Travers gave his particulars, which were written down.

"And monsieur desires also to protest?" asked the *agent* ironically.

"At the right time and place," Travers assured him. "Meanwhile, if it is by the orders of M. Gallois that you act, he is not unknown to me."

"In this life," the *agent* told him philosophically, "one is known to everyone else. That is an affair which will doubtless arrange itself. And now we will go. The apartment will be guarded till we return."

He waited while she fetched a hat and coat from the bedroom, and then the party of four made its way down. A car was standing by the door. Travers was instructed to sit in front with the driver, and another *agent* sat in the back between Charles and Elise. Then, to Travers's amazement, the first *agent* jumped on the running board, and the car moved off.

The three had been in the silence of the waiting-room for about five minutes when feet were heard in the passage outside, and the gendarme on duty went to the door. A voice was heard demanding M. Travers, and in a moment Travers was being shepherded along a corridor, and then a second, till a door was opened and he was in the room of Gallois.

Gallois came forward, hand outstretched, and there was a warmth in his smile.

"My friend, you forgive this comedy which it is still necessary that we should play? But I need you urgently and I ring your hotel, and madame your wife assures me that you have just departed with Charles to view a picture. And now you understand?"

"There's nothing to apologize for," smiled Travers. "But you wanted me urgently, you said?"

Gallois explained. That night at Fécamp had been a night of gales, and the papers reported more than one boat missing and lives lost. But that morning the body of a man had been washed ashore near St. Valéry, and Gallois wanted to take no risks. Even if it were a thousand to one against, he still wanted to be sure the man was not Bertrand.

"But M. Larne can identify Bertrand," pointed out Travers.

"Of that I am not sure," Gallois said. "This man wears a beard and he has not the appearance of Bertrand such as we imagine it. And even if M. Larne identifies the man as Bertrand Gurlot, that is not what we so urgently desire. What is important is that we discover if this drowned one was an associate of Braque, which is why I send for the woman Moulins."

Before the puzzled Travers could utter a word of comment, there was a rap at the door.

"Send the woman Moulins," Gallois said, and then was smiling Travers to a chair.

Almost at once Elise was encoring. Travers felt an overwhelming pity for her as she stood there with frightened eyes on Gallois. But Gallois was going to meet her, and his eyes had a pity too. He was distressed, he said, to disarrange her affairs, but all that was required of her was her help. There was a drowned one, an unfortunate who had been recovered by the police, and who might have been an associate of Braque. All that was desired was that she should look at him and say if she recalled his face.

His hand fell gently on her shoulder.

"It is an affair of perhaps a minute. All that then remains is to reconduct you to your apartment."

She was moistening her lips. She made as if to speak, and then was shaking her head.

"There is something you desire to say?" Gallois asked her gently.

She shook her head again, and then the words came.

"And M. Rabaud. He also has done nothing?"

"Nothing in the world," he assured her. "This gentleman explains your M. Rabaud. And now?"

He was leading her through the door and into the corridor. In a moment the three were in a bare room, where there was a table on which lay something covered with a sheet. A man whom Travers took to be a surgeon stood by it, and Gallois nodded to him as he came in. Then he was moving back the sheet from the head, and it was with eyes of horror that Travers saw the white emaciated face against the greyish black of the unkempt beard.

"Courage," Gallois said. "Approach, if you please. You recognize this man?"

She gave one nervous look and then was shaking her head.

"Regard once more," Gallois said gently. "You are surer"

She shook her head again.

Gallois drew back the sheet and nodded to the surgeon. Once more he took Elise by the arm as if to lead her away, then at the door he changed his mind.

"But I am an imbecile," he said, and rapped his skull with his knuckles. "This beard, it is perhaps grown within a week or two, and also it disguises the face. We will remove the beard and then perhaps one will be able to recognize. Meanwhile we will wait."

He moved on again. Elise cast a frightened look back at Travers, who smiled reassuringly. Gallois had yet another scheme in mind, he was thinking to himself, and like the others it appeared to him to have in it much of the unnecessary.

Back in the room Gallois excused himself to Travers and said he would return in a minute. Travers smiled across at Elise.

"There is no need to distress yourself," he told her. "It is only a formality which is necessary perhaps for all of us, and after that one is troubled no more by the police."

The thought seemed to cheer her, and there was a long silence in the room till the feet of Gallois at last were heard.

"Again one minute," he announced, "and everything is finished."

It was Travers now who took the arm of Elise, and he felt its nervous shaking and watched the quick moistening of her lips. Again the sheet was drawn back, and the face now appeared more emaciated than ever. Then Travers saw a something that made his eyes almost start from his head.

"C'est Maurice!"

She was scaring, fingers frightenedly at her mouth, and the cry was a kind of stifled shriek.

"Maurice?" said Gallois, eyes narrowing. "And who is this Maurice?"

But her feet seemed to give way and she was slithering to the floor. Travers was holding her at once, and the surgeon came across too. He whispered something to Gallois, who stooped and gathered her in his arms.

"You also know this Maurice?" he said to Travers.

"I'm not sure," Travers said, and was shaking his head bewilderedly. "But she was sure. That cut by the mouth that the Professor mentioned. The Laughing Man, he called him."

The lip of Gallois drooped.

"The Laughing Man. The brother who is dead for five years."

He shook his head again, and with Travers at his heels, moved off along the corridor.

CHAPTER XIV
THE DISCOVERY

IT WAS A QUARTER of an hour before Gallois came back to his room, and he announced that the woman had already recovered, and in a few minutes might be able to answer questions.

"But you understand now, do you not, why I do not ask M. Larne to do the identification?"

"Frankly, I don't," Travers said bluntly.

"But consider," expostulated Gallois. "I go and see this dead man. I know because of the beard that he cannot be Pierre, but there is a chance that he may be Gurlot. But when I examine the beard, I see the scar where the hair does not grow. I say to myself that there are not two men in all France with a mouth that is cut at the side, and I am astounded, like yourself, when I know that he is Moulins. Then I remember something else, that Braque was with Moulins at the Académie Poussin. I say to myself that we seek the members of the gang, and here perhaps is a member. But when I demand if this Moulins is also Bertrand Gurlot, then I begin to doubt.

"By example, M. Larne knew this Moulins. If he had for some reasons changed his name to Gurlot and married this Hortense, then at some time M. Larne would have seen and spoken with him, and he would have recognized Moulins. Also this Moulins would have recognized M. Larne. That is so, is it not?"

"I quite agree," Travers said. "But why not take a short cut to all this? Ring M. Larne at his hotel and ask him to describe Bertrand Gurlot as he was when he saw him last."

"An excellent idea!" exclaimed Gallois.

He pushed the buzzer and was asking for a connection to be made.

"While we attend," he went on, "I will also say this. You have seen this Moulins, and one can observe that he was a moribund. The doctors assure me that he was almost dead before he was drowned. Therefore he had not the strength to attack François, and he had not the strength to drive even the motor-boat or the car."

The bell went and he was picking the receiver up. Larne was on the phone, and Travers could take in the gist of the talk. Gallois was devastated at disturbing the great man, but since when was it that he had actually clapped eyes on Bertrand? Almost a year? That was indeed a long time. And the appearance of this Bertrand? Clean-shaven, tall, round-shouldered and with a high complexion, and in age about fifty? Bald, and slightly lame from an old war wound? That was an admirable description and ample, and before ringing off, Gallois uttered more apologies and thanks.

"You hear?" he said to Travers. "This Moulins is not the Bertrand Gurlot that we seek. Yet he is drowned, and not many kilometres from that house, and he was known to Braque." He shook his head. "There is a riddle to which I find no answer."

"Everything's been too sudden for me," Travers said. "I can't get that ghastly face out of my mind, let alone think. But there's another mystery that I can see arising. If a priest in Algiers sent word to Elise Moulins that her brother had died there, then who was it that died there? And since he wasn't Maurice Moulins, then how did he know that Elise existed?"

Gallois nodded. "That is something that also seems to me incredible. But to-day, like you, I am unable to think. Since I observe that body, my brain boils. Now all I can suggest is this. There was a Bertrand Gurlot, but he died or disappeared. Then one conceives the plan of bringing this Moulins to take his place, unknown to M. Larne, who was so often away from the Villa and for such long times."

"Now we're arriving at something," Travers said. "This Moulins needn't have known it, but he was a member of the gang. Braque ran across him when he was down-and-out somewhere, and he was used as a copyist of pictures. A producer of fakes, if you like."

Gallois nodded again. "And when M. Larne arrives for a stay at the Villa, then this Moulins is sick. But soon he becomes so ill that the truth cannot be hidden. It is necessary that he dies somewhere else, and so it is contrived that he dies at Fécamp."

He glanced at his watch, then got to his feet.

"If you had been at your hotel, you would have come here direct and we should have talked of these things before the arrival of the sister of Moulins. As it was, we must play once more a comedy which has the air of being ridiculous."

His tone changed to the confidential.

"To-night there are two questions with which I desire that you sleep, and in the morning it may be that you find the answers. We wonder, do we not, who it is that died at Algiers, and, since he is not the brother of Elise, how he could communicate to the priest a wish that one informed her of his death. We arrive then at the first question. *Was there ever a letter from this priest?*"

Travers's fingers were suddenly at his glasses.

"I wonder. I don't think anyone has ever seen the letter. She told me it was lost."

Gallois nodded ominously.

"The second question, it is this. *Why did she faint in that room?* At the sight of a brother whom she does not see for many years, and whom she remembers so little that she does not recognize till one has removed the beard? Does she faint because the dead one is alive, or because of a conscience which is guilty? And because she is afraid that now we know everything." He wagged a last dramatic finger. "Remember always that she was an associate of Braque."

Travers had to turn his head at the thought of it.

"It's horrible," he said. "Unbelievably horrible. To think that she knew all the time her brother was there, and should lend herself to making a tool of him."

Gallois smiled sadly.

"This evening she looks pathetic, does she not? One says to one's self that there is a mistake, and she is after all a woman of modesty and of a good heart. It is impossible that she tells a lie, or is other than a victim of what one calls mischance." He shook his head with the same mournful smile. "But I have known women like that, who have been capable of everything: of lies, of murder, of everything which is a crime."

"All the same, she didn't kill Braque," Travers said. "And her brother didn't kill him. As far as I can see now, the only possible assassin left is Hortense."

"Or this Bertrand who disappears and is replaced by Moulins." Then his hand went out. "Good night, my friend. To-morrow you find an answer to the questions. I commence to enquire in my own way into the disappearance of Bertrand Gurlot."

Then he was halting at the door.

"An idea also comes. There is always the evidence which M. Larne can give, but which he keeps so closely to himself. It would be possible, do you think, that to-morrow you arrange to see M. Larne? You bring him only what one calls gossip. He will be astonished, you think, to hear that one has found drowned this Moulins whom he also knew at the Académie Poussin, and you will say also that it is curious that he is drowned so near to Fécamp. If you wish, you say also that I, Gallois, am at Fécamp to make enquiries, and that to you I give the impression that there are things which I soon discover."

"I see," said Travers slowly. "There's a good deal we both suspect that he knows, and that might force his hand."

Gallois clapped him on the shoulder.

"My friend, you are the second brain of myself. And it is not only what he says that you observe. It is also the eyes, and the movements, because it is them that he thinks you do not observe."

Then, as he held out his hand again, his smile was even more melancholy and apologetic.

"There are times, are there not, when to one so calm, so phlegmatic as yourself, my friend, this Gallois has an air of the theatrical. To-night, perhaps, you wonder why we play the comedy at the apartment of the woman. But one suspicion, and she also disappears perhaps, like the others, and then it is for her also that we must search."

Travers smiled the least bit sheepishly. Gallois had once more uncannily read his thoughts, and in a moment he was admitting generously that his own ideas had been altogether wrong.

But Travers awoke in the morning with a feeling of uneasiness in his mind, and in a moment he was knowing what it was.

It was not that he had seen in his dreams the ghastly emaciated face of the dead Moulins, but the remembering of that interview which he must have with Larne.

Duplicity of that kind was the one form of detection for which he had a tremendous aversion. To be an off-hand and occasional liar was something which he knew to be most necessary, and when one was dealing with those who also were liars, then the battle of wits had its amusing side. But what he disliked was to pose and lie to those for whom he had a respect, and who, above all, had an implicit confidence in himself. But by breakfast he could assure himself that what he was about to do would be for Larne's own good, and the very moment Bernice had gone, he would hurry along to Larne and get things over.

Bernice was spending what she said was positively the last day of widowhood, and she would be back before dinner. Her friends arrived for her soon after ten o'clock, and it was half an hour later before the party left. Then Travers jotted down the lines he wished the talk with Larne to follow, and, with courage screwed to the sticking point, rang the hotel.

But M. Larne was out, he was told, and he would not be back till the early evening. Travers, disappointed at so much effort for nothing, asked if the hotel would ring him should Larne make an earlier return. Then he rang Gallois to report the putting off of the interview, but Gallois was out and was not expected back till the afternoon. The whereabouts of M. Rabaud, they said, were unknown.

Travers, considering himself legitimately free, spent the rest of the morning in an antique shop, then, after lunch, tied down by the knowledge that Larne's hotel might report his earlier return, amused himself by trying to review the case.

What he wished above all was to simplify things: to untie all the knots with which the clear line of thought was hampered and involved, and to make of the case a something which was simplicity itself to follow. Soon he was getting paper and writing down the ideas that came.

Assume, he began, that there was some criminal scheme to make money. Braque called it a gold-mine, and for the moment one might disregard whether or not there were two gold-mines and if the second was really a development of, and an improvement on, the first.

ORIGINAL MEMBERS OF THE GANG. That was his headline, and under it he wrote the names of Braque, Pierre Larne, Bertrand Gurlot and Hortense Gurlot. Henri Larne, he noted, was so often away from the Villa that the gang had practically a free hand there.

SECOND PHASE. Braque ran across the derelict Moulins, and suggested him as a useful member of the gang. He was given the name of Gurlot, and doubtless knew little of what was going on, as he would be drunk most of the time. Bertrand Gurlot was set free to be employed in Spain or wherever the activities of the gang requited him.

And there Travers was delighted to find the solution to one mystery that had puzzled him all along—who it was or rather why it was that an attack had been made on Larne's life. The reason, he now saw, was this. Moulins had become desperately ill. The gang were in a panic, and a solution seemed to be to remove Larne. But the plan failed, and it was decided instead that Moulins should be removed from the Villa, so that if he died suddenly then his body might be surreptitiously disposed of.

It was getting well on in the afternoon by the time Travers had arrived at that, and all that seemed left to do was to find what still failed to fit in. And there at once he was up against the question of Elise Moulins. If the suspicions of Gallois were correct, how was she to be accounted for? Had she been an associate of Braque for much longer than she had admitted? Was it she who proposed that the gang might use the talent of her brother? If not, what had been her functions as a useful member?

Travers had an early tea, then rang Larne's hotel. But Larne had not returned, and he settled again to an examination of

Elise Moulins. But theory seemed for once inadequate, and he was wondering if he could contrive to talk with her again. If she had been playing the fiendish part that Gallois assigned to her, then, thought Travers, she was an actress of the very front rank. Even under the watchful eyes of Charles, she had played her part. Only a great actress could pretend that revulsion of feeling towards Braque, and the remnants of love for a dead brother, of all of which that picture in her kitchen had been a kind of symbol. And there had been that pathetic, artless remark of the previous night—"And M. Rabaud, he also has done nothing?"— when all the time perhaps she was only too well aware of the comedy that was being played.

Then Travers was suddenly annoyed with Charles for not putting in an appearance. If he arrived he could be asked to arrange another interview with Elise. With that, Travers put the case aside and went on with his book. But Charles did not arrive, and suddenly Travers was putting the book aside. Charles was possibly at the apartment of Elise, and he himself would go there and, as excuse, resume the talk about the picture where the arrival of the police had interrupted it.

So Travers called a taxi and asked to be set down at the end of the rue Vagnolles. Dusk was in the sky, but with the little light that there was, the neighbourhood seemed less unsavoury, and it even had a kind of friendliness that was forlorn. There were people about, which also made a difference, and it was with a feeling of unreality that he opened that side door and began to mount the stairs.

It was dark there, and on the first landing he switched on the light. Then suddenly the door above him opened, and the head of Charles appeared. A startled look, and Charles was putting his finger to his lips, and closing the door quietly behind him, and making signs for Travers to descend again.

"It is necessary that I explain," he said. "Last night she was distressed and ill, but this morning she is better, but she refuses to go out. I say it is better she keeps the appointment that she has, because when one works, one forgets. So she goes out, and I go also, and she imagines it is to you. Then I return and she is here, and I say that I ask for the evening to be free for me as she is upset about her brother."

A voice was heard calling him from above. Once more his fingers went to his lips.

"I go now to explain that I descend and meet monsieur by chance. Meanwhile she prepares. It is about the picture that you come?"

Travers nodded, but already Charles was running up the stairs. In two minutes be appeared again, and was making signs for Travers to ascend.

The little kitchen seemed as spotless as ever. Elise was regarding him with no suspicions.

"I am sorry to disturb you again," Travers began.

There was a genuineness about her quiet smile.

"Monsieur is very good. It was not right that Charles should make him wait."

"But it is an intrusion," he told her. "But now I am here, I come for two things: to see the picture again and to express my condolences about your brother. It was a great shock."

She said nothing for a moment, then shook her head.

"Monsieur is very good."

Travers was feeling the least bit ill at ease. Conversation was becoming hard to make.

"It was a shock to me," he went on, "to hear that it was your brother. But how was it that one imagined him dead?"

Charles cut in there with an explanation. If monsieur permitted, he would suggest that when Maurice was in Algiers he was robbed, and it was the thief who had met some sudden end. In the thief's pocket were found papers mentioning the name of Maurice and of Elise.

"That is doubtless the explanation," Travers said. "All the same, it was foolish for the police to imagine your brother was the associate of criminals and scoundrels."

"The police, if monsieur permits, are fools and pigs," said Charles.

Elise was smiling sadly.

"But my brother was—was like my father. He was the friend of anyone who would buy a drink."

"But that is no disgrace to yourself," Travers told her, eyes on her downcast face and the hands so absurdly placid in her lap. "One regrets the doings of one's relatives but one is not responsible. For yourself there is nothing but a credit that you maintain yourself all these years. But the picture; you still wish that I buy it?"

She thought for a moment, then slowly shook her head.

"If monsieur is not offended, I think that perhaps I will keep it."

Travers nodded gravely.

"I understand. But you will permit that I examine it more closely?"

She smiled at that and Charles was at once taking it off its nail. Travers polished his glasses and placed the picture beneath the light.

Quick, bold work, he thought, with a really masterly passage where the light came by the neck and chin. The portrait of some chance cabaret or country client doubtless, and executed for a few sous. Then the sitter had indignantly refused it as far from his conceptions both of himself and of a coloured photograph, and the painter had had it left on his hands.

Yet Travers was somehow fascinated, and by those grim associations with that white, emaciated face he had seen on that bare table at the Sûreté. Curious work, he thought, like that of a man who has yet to find himself. Crude in its background—

And then Travers was all at once fumbling for his glasses. As he slowly polished them, eyes blinking beneath the light, the two were watching him and wondering what had happened to make him frown to himself and shake his head.

"It is a picture I would like at some time to possess," he all at once said. "If at any time you should wish to sell, it would be a favour if it was to me that you gave the opportunity to buy."

He had spoken the stilted words, and yet the voice seemed distant and not his own. Methodically he picked up his hat, and yet he made no move to go.

"There is something that monsieur desires?"

Charles's voice brought him somehow to himself.

"Yes," he said. "I regret to change my mind but for an hour I shall need you at the hotel. After that you are free."

He smiled a grave good night to Elise and slowly and thoughtfully made his way down the stairs. In a moment Charles was pattering after him. The taxi was waiting and in five minutes they were at the hotel. Once more the taxi was told to wait, and Travers went up to his rooms.

Bernice was not yet back, and he telephoned at once to Larne's hotel. Larne had just that moment come in, they said, and the message should be delivered at once.

"Tell him that I arrive in five minutes, and that it is urgent," repeated Travers, and hung up.

Next he wrote a message for Bernice, placed it where she could not fail to see it, and was nodding to Charles to accompany him downstairs again.

"You will remain here in the lobby," he said. "If madame arrives, it does not affect the order. In half an hour I shall be back, and then perhaps there will be things that we have to do."

Another minute and the taxi was taking him towards Larne's hotel, and all that he could think of was one thing. Within an hour—or it might possibly be two—he would know for a certainty who it was that had murdered Braque.

CHAPTER XV
THE RUE VAGNOLLES

LARNE CAME FORWARD, hand outstretched, but there was an obvious anxiety in his smile.

"How are you? It's very nice to see you again." And before Travers could say a word, "You've got some news for me?"

"I'm afraid I haven't," Travers said. "I want your help in a certain matter, that's all."

"Sit down," Larne said. "What may I offer you? There's a very excellent sherry."

"Thank you, perhaps I will," Travers told him. "And I'll sit down for a minute or two. This talk, by the way, is extremely confidential."

Larne poured out the two sherries and then drew up a chair to face him.

"Confidential? You mean that it's nothing to do with all this deplorable business of the last few days?"

"Unhappily it has everything to do with it," Travers said. "I hope for one thing that it will settle the whole matter up. But you won't mind my referring again to your brother? I want to know, for instance, if you have any reason to suspect that there was any relationship between your brother and the model, Elise Deschamps."

Larne looked puzzled, then a different look came over his face. It was as if he remembered, and then decided to again forget.

"I can't possibly imagine anything of the kind," he said. "But how does it affect all this business?"

"Well"—Travers thought things out for a moment—"perhaps I'd better be very blunt. You have been forced to admit that your brother was a connection of Braque, and this Elise Deschamps was a connection too. How deeply she was involved we—and there I mean the Inspector Gallois—didn't realize till certain new information came to hand to-day. Some has only just reached me, and it's what I've discovered for myself. That's why

I'm communicating it to you privately." He smiled. "I'm afraid I'm becoming rather involved. What I want to say is this. If both your brother and the woman Deschamps were associates—and close associates—of Braque, then they should have been well known to each other."

"It's possible," Larne said slowly. "But whatever was going on, I was unaware of it myself." He looked up. "But what is this private information of yours?"

"Perhaps I'd better begin at the beginning," Travers said. "You know how the woman—we'll call her Elise—how Elise claimed to have become acquainted with Braque?"

"If I ever did know, I've forgotten it."

"Well, she says her brother—who was the Moulins you knew at the Académie Poussin—gave her, or left behind, one of his pictures just before he disappeared. She offered the picture to Braque, just as one tries to sell a picture to a dealer, and he didn't want it. He made certain other suggestions instead by which she could raise money. Then later he was interested very much in the picture but she wouldn't sell it. All this is quite recent history, by the way."

"A picture by Moulins," Larne said reflectively. "Let me see. What was his other name? It's on the tip of my tongue."

"Maurice," Travers said. "That's what the sister said. Also I had occasion to see the picture, and it's signed like that."

"It's signed 'Maurice Moulins'?"

"Well, no," Travers said. "Only the initials. But what I'm driving at is that his name was Maurice, not that it matters. But about that picture, which is really a sketch in oils or a quick portrait of a man. There it hangs in her kitchen, and she's supposed to have been treasuring it for years as a memento of a dead brother. You remember that I told you he died in Algiers five years or more ago, and she was supposed to have had a letter about it." He leaned forward. "Well, the keeping of that picture was all humbug. Maurice Moulins didn't die five years ago. His body was washed ashore only a day ago."

"Washed ashore!"

"Yes, and very near Fécamp. And now do you see the point?"

But Larne had got to his feet and was pacing restlessly about the room.

"But how on earth could a man like this dead Moulins have any connection with my brother, and going to Fécamp?"

"That's what I want to find out," Travers said. "It's also what Gallois is now hoping to find out at Fécamp. You see, the whole thing does not hang together. Your brother and this Elise and Braque all mixed up in something shady, and to do with the pictures, and then the brother is found dead near Fécamp of all places. Excuse me if I emphasize that. The brother of Elise, and he also happens to be a painter! Things are getting beyond mere coincidence, and I think you must agree."

Larne came back to his chair with a question.

"Yes, but are you sure it was Moulins who was drowned?"

"The sister herself identified him last night," Travers said. "I've been trying to get you all day to tell you so."

Larne's head went forward between his cupped hands, and then as suddenly he had an idea.

"Yes, but what explanations did the sister give when the police interrogated her?"

"She said nothing," Travers told him. "The police can't get anything out of her. All she does is stick to her original story. *But,* here's the point." He looked at his watch. "In another half-hour or so, she will be interrogated again, and much more closely. That's why I came to you with the hope of getting private information. It could be kept private if you so desired it, but it would be a big weapon in our hands to know it."

Larne shrugged his shoulders helplessly.

"But what information can I give?"

The smile of Travers had a sadness reminiscent of Gallois.

"Why do you think I'm doing all this unknown to the police? You told me certain things in confidence, which you didn't wish the police to know. You were shielding your brother, and you and I might as well admit the fact."

"I've washed my hands of him," Larne said fiercely. "To-morrow night I sail for America. If he follows me there, then I shall tell what I know, and not before."

"But consider," said Travers earnestly. "If the police suspect—and I come here to say that they do already begin to suspect—that you are withholding information, they will request you to remain here till everything is cleared up. You don't want that, and I think I can avoid it."

"But what information can I give?" Larne asked exasperatedly.

"Information about Elise Deschamps," Travers said quietly. "Information which will remain a confidence between you and me."

Larne got to his feet, hands quivering.

"But I know nothing about the woman!"

"Sit down, please," Travers told him gently. "Let me point out something. Was it not a curious coincidence that this woman who, I'm almost certain, knew your brother, should present herself here that evening as your model?"

Larne was looking interested, then shook his head.

"It is possible that she could have arranged it herself. But if she did, what difference does it make?"

"This," said Travers. "It may establish the one fact which will be the end of all this business. *The fact that it was she who murdered Braque.*"

Larne stared.

"But she couldn't! Unless the police have been lying?"

"How do you mean?"

"Wasn't I informed that Braque was murdered at a quarter to six that night?"

"Braque *was* murdered at a quarter to six."

"But I had her beneath my eyes from long before that till long after it!"

Once more Travers smiled sadly.

"Are you sure? Now you come to think things out, *are you sure?*"

"What do you mean?"

Larne was once more on his feet, hands quivering indignantly. Then he was turning away again. There was a chair in the far corner, and he made his way to it, and sat there, head bowed in his hands.

"Whatever I tell you will be between you and me?" he said at last.

"You have my word," said Travers simply.

"Very well then." He came back to his old chair. "The trouble is, I don't think you'll believe me."

"You needn't fear that," Travers told him.

"But I can't believe it myself. I never have believed it, even when I thought I had it worked out." Then he was making a gesture of annoyance. "If we could go to the Villa, then perhaps it would be easier. But everything there has gone. That is what I have been busy about to-day—that and other things."

"I remember the studio perfectly," Travers reminded hint.

"Of course," he said, surprisedly. "And you were there that evening. You remember how she pretended to be very tired, and said she had already given two sittings?"

Travers nodded.

"And then I said that she might refresh herself by making a cup of tea, and one for me also." He was leaning forward impressively. "This is what happened. You departed, and I was anxious to begin. While the kettle boiled I explained to her the precise pose, and then she made the tea and brought a cup for me and one for herself. Hers she had in the very chair where she would pose. I sat for a moment by the easel, and I slowly drank my tea while I studied the light. It was an easy chair in which I sat. You remember it?"

"Perfectly."

"Then in a minute it seemed to me that I had been asleep. Just a doze, perhaps, for I had spent an anxious day, and I have the facility to fall asleep in a moment. I glanced at the clock, which stood, if you remember, on the mantelpiece beneath my eye—"

"Behind the model's back."

"Exactly! I glanced at the clock and I had not slept for more than a minute, for she was still drinking her tea. After that I worked furiously, as you know, and it was only later that I felt a strange taste in my mouth."

Travers nodded.

"It had to be like that," he said. "I was sure of it. But there's still something else. She drugged your tea and you slept till she had returned from the rue Jourdoise. She stopped the clock while you slept and when she returned she started it again. But if your brother arrived at the Villa at about the same time in the car, wouldn't he have seen her?"

Larne was motionless for a long half-minute, then he nodded.

"Very well then, I will tell you. I think that the car which I heard was heard when I was almost asleep. I think now that it was my brother's car which she—or both of them—used. And there is something even more strange. You will not believe it, but I will try to explain. When one wakes, one is not immediately awake. It is like the second or two when one begins to recover from gas after a tooth has been pulled out. Well, just as I was in the act of waking, I seemed to see my brother in the room and to hear him speak. Then I was really awake and I thought naturally I'd had a short nap and dreamed the whole thing."

Travers sprang to his feet and glanced at his watch again.

"That's everything I want to know. The woman will be examined at once. I may be there, and I may put a question or two to her which no one but myself and she will understand. Or I may question her later, when the police have finished, at her apartment in the rue Vagnolles."

"You will be discreet?" Larne was asking urgently.

"I will be more than discreet," Travers assured him. "Your name, you can rest assured, shall never be even mentioned."

"You will tell me what happens?"

"Most decidedly I will," Travers assured him. "And now I must hurry away. Inside ten minutes she ought to be under arrest and taken to the Sûreté. We know just where she is."

Larne was still somewhat diffident.

"But what can you do without my evidence?"

Travers smiled. "The police have their own methods, which you and I aren't allowed to enquire into too closely. And I promise you this on my word of honour. You'll not be required to give evidence at her trial or at any time. As far as she's concerned, you cease to exist. Is that good enough?"

Larne expressed himself as completely satisfied.

Travers gave the driver no order to hurry. His plans were not yet fully made, and before the hotel was reached again, he needed time for thought. And the speed of things had thrown him somewhat out of gear. He had formed a theory and he had hoped, but hopes had turned out incredibly better than his most optimistic anticipation and now he had to plan accordingly.

First, he thought, he must tell Gallois everything he had discovered. And there he paused. Gallois had set a fashion in secrecy, and it would do him no harm to be given a dose of his own prescription.

Charles reported that madame had arrived immediately after Travers's departure. Travers said the note he had left would be sufficient to explain an absence, however long, and that he and Charles were off on an expedition. Meanwhile there was a brief phone-call to make.

It was Gallois whom he rang, and Gallois himself who answered.

"Ah, my friend, you have seen M. Larne?"

"Yes," said Travers, "but I will tell you all about that later. And now—"

"You have found the answers to the questions? The questions I gave to you last night?"

"Yes," Travers said. "And I want you to do this at once. It's a matter of extreme urgency. You understand? Extremely urgent and to be done at once. Arrest Elise Moulins and take her to the Sûreté."

"Arrest Elise Moulins and take her to the Sûreté," Gallois said as if to himself. "Very well, my friend. I have confidence in you to know that you have reasons. In fifteen minutes she shall be here. And you?"

"I shall arrive when I do arrive," Travers said. "Don't be alarmed if it's not for some time. And don't ring the hotel because I shan't be here."

He gave a quick good-bye and rang off. Then Charles was informed that they were going back to the rue Vagnolles, and by taxi.

But well short of that back street, Travers stopped the taxi and paid the driver off.

"Is there a way to come in at the other end of the street?" he asked Charles.

Charles was moving off at once and in three minutes was announcing that they had just turned into the rue Vagnolles.

"And where is number thirty-one?" Travers wanted to know.

Charles indicated a sign that jutted over the road about a hundred yards away. Travers also remembered that it was practically opposite the apartment.

"We will go closer," he said, and began making his way towards it. And then all at once a car appeared in the street. It drew up at that side door, and Travers was grabbing the arm of Charles and drawing him back into the darkness.

"Watch," he said, "and make no move. Whatever happens, don't stir."

Three men had got out of the car, and one disappeared through the side door. Through the dull windows the landing lights were seen to go on, but it was almost five minutes before the man appeared again, and with him was a woman who entered the car. In a flash the other two men were in, the car backed, and with a whirl of gears was gone again.

"There is another interrogation?" Charles said.

"Yes," Travers told him. "There are things that have just been discovered. It appears that she was concerned in the murder of this Braque."

"But, monsieur, it is impossible," Charles said fiercely.

"One must not say that," Travers told him quietly. "It is not for us to question the orders of M. Gallois."

"It is he?" demanded Charles with the same indignation. "Then he is an imbecile. I could have told him—"

He was suddenly quiet, and shaking his head.

"Told him what?"

"It is nothing," Charles said despondently. "But I know her, and I know that she is incapable of this thing."

"Well, you'll have your chance to say what you know," Travers told him.

"We will go, then—"

Travers held him by the arm.

"We remain here, and for once you act under my instructions. And, no talking. All we have to do is watch."

Then Travers saw something he had not noticed, that a man had emerged from the side door. The bad light had deceived him and now he realized that a man must have been placed on guard while the woman was absent.

"Listen," said Travers. "All these *agents* are known to you?"

"Doubtless," Charles said laconically, and there was still a grievance in his tone.

"Then tell that man that you have the orders of M. Gallois. He is to remove himself over there, just out of that light, and you will stay with him and keep the door under observation. It is important that neither of you should be observed. You understand that? If anything miscarries, I hold you responsible. Remain there no matter how long. It anyone enters the door, make no move, but when he comes out, wait till he is near you and then arrest him. If he comes this way, I will stop him. If he arrives by taxi, then close in on the taxi as soon as he re-enters."

"Ah!" said Charles. "This Pierre Larne returns?"

"Yes," said Travers. "It appears that he returns."

Another two minutes and that gloomy street was deserted again.

Travers lighted a cigarette and shielded it while he smoked, and his eyes were always on that door. Twice there were people who appeared, but they had no business at that door. Half an hour went by, and nothing happened, and then a man appeared at the far end by which Travers and Charles had come. He was a tall man, and lame, and he looked about him as he slowly made his way along that ill-lighted street. Then he crossed to that side where Travers was, and Travers drew quietly back to the darkness of his concealing doorway. Then all at once the lameness of the man had gone, and he was at Travers's elbow.

"It is you, my friend?"

"Yes," whispered Travers, "But how did you know I was here?"

Gallois was now in the same shelter of the doorway.

"Perhaps I have what one calls the intuition. This morning, by example, Pierre Larne arrives in Paris. What is more natural than that he should come here when it is dark to arrange with this Elise Moulins with whom he is so acquaint?"

"You've questioned him?" asked the startled Travers.

But the fingers of Gallois had closed all at once about his arm, and the narrow street had suddenly an oppressive quiet. A man was coming slowly towards the door, and his rubber-shod boots made no sound on the cobbles. He passed the door, still walking slowly, and then twenty yards on, he turned. He approached that door again, and then as if by some queer illusion, he had suddenly disappeared.

Travers was motionless, Gallois waited a moment.

"Allons!" he said, but the hand of Travers drew him back.

"Remain here!" he said. "All the precautions are taken. It is necessary that we wait till he emerges."

There were no lights that flashed on below the stairs, and the man might have been some delusion of the brain. But for the sound of their own quiet breathing, the street had still a silence that was strangely oppressive. Then, before they were scarcely aware, there was a darkness by the doorway. The man appeared again, and there seemed a difference about his shape, but it was only a something he was carrying. A quick look each way along that gloomy street and he was crossing to the other side.

Travers moved and Gallois with him. They moved more quickly and broke into a run, and ahead of them there was a cry and the sound of more feet on the damp cobble-stones. Gallois was now running madly, and then as suddenly he halted. Travers drew pantingly up to see him standing with Charles and the other man, looking down at a figure that sprawled on the scones.

"He hasn't killed himself?"

"No," said Charles. "It was the wet of the stones, and he slipped, and he struck perhaps his head."

He was stooping and feeling, and turning the man to the light. Then his voice came startledly.

"But it is not Pierre!" His mouth had a foolish gape. "It is the painter—Henri Larne! Where then is Pierre?"

"That I know," said Gallois unconcernedly. "Since five o'clock, Pierre has been under arrest."

"You know everything!" asked the bewildered Travers.

Gallois shook his head.

"No, my friend. This Pierre refuses to speak." He shrugged his shoulders. "There is very little that I know. At this moment I do not even know for a certainty who it was that killed Braque. And if I guess, then it is incredible how it could be done."

But Travers was picking up that awkward-looking thing that had fallen from the grasp of the slipping man.

"Ah! the picture," Gallois said. "It is of an importance?"

"Yes," said Travers. "It is everything that one needs. On it you will read what it is that will end this case—the name of the man who killed Braque."

CHAPTER XVI
THE FLYING DONKEY

GALLOIS HAD INSISTED that Travers should be first with the explanation. Charles was in the room too, though Elise was doubtless imagining that he had been removed for interrogation. It was Travers who had insisted that the comedy should be played to its end, and Charles had at first been sent to the room where she waited.

"Though I didn't know it," began Travers, "what was always at the back of my mind was a feeling of disappointment which I could never quite explain. Now I know that it was this: I never felt we had a satisfactory explanation for that curious conduct of Braque in the Tate Gallery that morning I told you about. But we'll come to that later. What I'll do is begin at where the whole scheme began, and if you think I'm wrong"—he paused to smile—"or know I'm wrong, then you'll tell me.

"To begin with Henri Larne. He was a good portrait painter of the humdrum kind, and he realized he'd never do more than scrape a living in France. So he went to America, where his mother's relations lived. Then, six years or so ago, and whether in America or France or even Algiers I can't say, he ran across the derelict Moulins. He couldn't help recognizing him, and I'd say that out of the kindness of his heart he befriended him and got him somewhat on his feet again. Moulins painted a picture or two—the still-life things that were now his speciality—and Larne must have gasped in amazement when he saw them. And what he decided to do was to try and market the pictures and pocket most of the proceeds. Then he thought of a much better scheme. He would pass the pictures off as his own. The only trouble was that Moulins had signed them with his initials, and to scrape off the pigment or tamper with it, might be suspicious.

"Then he had a far better scheme. He had never forgotten the jibe of a certain critic and the pun on his name, and he suddenly realized he could add additional strokes to the initials of Maurice Moulins' name. That was done like this, as you see on the picture he gave to his sister.

"That double M, artistically placed, was his signature. Now look at the picture he gave me, and you can see where the additional lines were added. Mind you, Moulins might not have gone on signing the pictures, but once Larne had taken the flying donkey for his signature, he had to go on with it, even if he painted the whole flying donkey himself— which wouldn't worry him at all. It would avoid all possibility of detection, for one thing. Have a look at this marguerite study he gave me, and compare. Most ingenious, don't you think?"

"Yes," said Gallois, after a long look. "That was undoubtedly the scheme. And yet this Henri Larne could never have killed Braque."

"That we shall see," Travers told him. "But to go back. The first picture so exhibited created a sensation at the Salon. Larne knew he had a gold-mine, and he decided to control its output. He gave Moulins every facility for drinking again—"

"You will pardon," broke in Gallois, "but you have not, as I have, the doctors' report. There may have been these facilities for drink, but it was drugs that they gave him. Everywhere on his arms are the pricks of the needle."

Travers winced. "Even more hellish than I thought. But the rest of the scheme is easy. Pierre, the half-brother, was brought into it, and the woman Gurlot to be the guardian and the supposed wife. A suitable retreat had to be found, and a most excellent one was discovered at the Villa Claire. Larne was supposed to paint very little, but it was Moulins who could only be induced to recover from the necessary drugs and paint little. But that didn't matter so much. It even in a way enhanced the value of what was saleable, and it helped to create a Larne legend.

"A letter, ostensibly written by a priest, was sent from Algiers to the sister whom Moulins must have mentioned to Larne, and the scheme settled down to steady working. For five years Moulins was kept alive, but of late he produced less and less that was really saleable. Owing to the drugs, he was less and less able to concentrate, and Larne had a dozen and more comparatively useless things of his which he explained away to me as being merely experiments in light.

"Then came the meeting of Braque and Élise Moulins. Braque saw nothing in the picture at first. Remember that both those signatures are very small, and the similarity didn't strike him till later. His first gold-mine in Spain had petered out, but now he knew he had a better one. Perhaps he privately watched the Villa, and he certainly made a close study of every signature of Larne's he could find—as he did that morning in the Tate—and be was anxious also to know what Larne was making out of the imposture. All that explains what he did in England, and the fact must remain that between the time I saw him and the time of my arrival in Paris, he had Larne under his thumb and was blackmailing him. Pierre was the go-between. It was from Larne that Braque got the wad of notes he flourished under the eyes of Cointeau. It was the Villa Claire that was the gold-mine to which, as Braque remarked to Cointeau, one had merely to take a taxi to reach."

"That, without doubt, is correct," said Gallois, and nodded. "All this money from the gold-mine of Moulins was now to be divided, not by two but by three."

"And there was the possibility that Braque would take far more than a third," Travers said. "I'd say the brothers resolved to get rid of him at once. Before he was actually murdered, Pierre was looking for likely houses where Moulins could be hidden again and more securely. But the real bomb-shell was when I artlessly appeared at the Villa Claire with my story of Braque in England.

"Larne told me a cock-and-bull story, about a burglary and an attempt to murder him—all to throw a veil of mystery round Braque and also himself, and he was most anxious to find out not only all I knew but all I was likely to know. Then on that Monday afternoon he began to see how he could use an innocent-looking amateur like myself to establish a perfect alibi. He pretended, for instance, that I had given him the inspiration he needed to paint a picture."

"You do not yet tell us of this alibi," Gallois said anxiously.

"I'm coming to it now," Travers said. "As an alibi, it was one of the best I've ever encountered. At five-thirty he began on blank canvas, and from then on he painted under the eyes of a model. Furthermore, when you and I arrived later, we knew from the vast amount of work he'd done that he must have concentrated with a tremendous intensity. Yet meanwhile he'd murdered Braque, and helped himself to the wad of notes with which he'd recently parted, and searched the rooms for anything incriminating.

"Next day I was told the story of Bertrand and how he was going to Grenoble, and how Larne had had his patience exhausted and was getting rid of Pierre. The rest of that you know better than I do."

"Yes," said Gallois. "But the murder, my friend. How was it committed? And how could you discover?"

"As soon as I clapped eyes on the initials in the corner of the sister's picture, that was how and when I discovered things," Travers said. "I saw the initials and there was also some curious recalling of Larne's pictures. Then, as soon as I began to work things out, I knew he must have done the murder. But even then I couldn't think how, and so I decided to put up a bluff and make him reveal it himself. When I saw him this evening I said we knew Elise had committed the murder but we couldn't discover how. I said she must have left the room for twenty minutes without his knowing it. Then he told me a story about her drugging the tea she made, and altering the clock, I can tell you his story later, but it's full of the most obvious flaws, but the main thing is that while he did incriminate Elise, he told me just what I wanted to know and incriminated himself. And as a final proof, I'd told him about the picture she had, and its connection with Braque, and how it had her brother's initials. I told him enough to make him aware that that picture must be got rid of. Then I made it easy by telling him in so many words that her apartment would be deserted. After that there was only to keep him under observation. He couldn't harm Elise because she was safely here, but he did take the picture."

He smiled as he caught Gallois' look of anxious impatience.

"But you want to hear how the alibi was worked. Well, it was planned with an ingenuity that was absolutely uncanny. On the murder morning he took a last precaution. He saw Cointeau, who didn't know him, and by means of shrewd questioning convinced himself that what Braque had already assured him was true—that Cointeau knew nothing of a secret which Braque was only too anxious to keep to himself. Next Larne rang me, pretending to be Braque, and arranged for me to go to the rue Jourdoise at six o'clock. Meanwhile he'd asked me to see him at the Villa where I was to establish his alibi.

"The picture of the Lazy Servant—shall we call it?—was of course already painted by Moulins, and all Larne was proposing was to adapt it and include a figure as a background to Moulins' simple still-life painting of vegetables. The pose, *and this is most important*, was designed so that the model should be in the most natural—and the most comfortable—position for sleep. The canvas I saw was a prepared blank, and while I was there the model arrived.

"You, my dear Gallois, had the idea that the secretary at the bureau wasn't telling you the truth when she said it was by accident that Elise Moulins went to the studio. Larne must have known all about Elise, of course, since he wrote that letter from Algiers, but all the same it doesn't matter now whether he wanted her specially as his model so as to be able to throw suspicion on her if need arose.

"What does not matter either is that Elise was tired and he told her to make tea. He'd have told her that in any case. She, or he, made the tea, and it was mildly drugged. He took care that she had finished drinking it just as he began to work. Then, if you remember, she was lying in a position of rest and at once she felt asleep, just as she was supposed to in the picture. Pierre, who was handy, came in to keep guard and to explain things plausibly if she awoke too soon. In twenty minutes at the latest, Larne was back. The clock, which stood *behind* the model, was put right and the finished canvas of Moulins—but for the figure—was put on the easel. Pierre disappeared and Larne began to paint in the model. She woke, and knew she had had a nap. But a peep disclosed that Larne had observed nothing. He had assumed she was merely posing, had never suspected a real sleep, and the last thing she would wish to do was to call attention to her lapse.

"On went Larne with his painting, which of course she couldn't see, and which was really a filling in of herself as a background and very roughly, as it would presumably have been done by Moulins. Then we arrived, and even if we had had suspicions, we should have known by the amount of work he'd done that he could never have left the room. That was the alibi, and I think you'll agree it was perfect."

"But for you, monsieur," said Charles, who had been straining hard to follow Travers's English.

"But for M. Travers, there you are right," said Gallois, with a majestic wave of the hand. "This is an example for one so inexperienced as yourself, to see how a master can employ his brain and his sensibility."

He was coming round from the table to shake Travers warmly by the hand.

"And you," said Travers. "There are things which you also must explain."

Gallois shrugged his shoulders. "Of myself I have a shame that is immense. It is you who are the artist, and I, I am what you call—what you call"

"A very modest fellow," broke in Travers "This was a partnership affair, and it's got to end up as one. It's your turn to do the explaining."

"Ah, well," said Gallois, and went back to his desk. "To explain, but what am I to explain? From the beginning I know everything, except what it is necessary that I should know. I know of the existence of this picture which is painted by Maurice Moulins, but to me, to me who claim that he is an artist, it showed nothing." He spread his palms with an enormous humility. "But I will also commence at the beginning.

"And it is at this very beginning that you assure me of something which is of the most interesting. There are three people who know the hotel at which you stay, and of the three I am one. Therefore I suspect the other two, who are Henri Larne and Pierre Larne. But Henri Larne, for many reasons and for his alibi, it is impossible to suspect seriously. There remains therefore that it was Pierre Larne who makes for you in the voice of Braque the appointment in the rue Jourdoise. There I was wrong, but the logic to me is still unanswerable. From the time that I suspect this Pierre to be the assassin of Braque, he is as far as possible under observation. Unhappily he was not followed to Fécamp when he came to see M. Archon just after the murder of Braque, because I had not begun sufficiently to suspect."

He made as if to continue, then shook his head.

"And now it becomes difficult for me to explain. Only the greatest of necessities would have made me commit such a—how do you say?—a thing so unpardonable, but to me it seemed such a necessity that I should conceal from you, my friend, many things which I do. But I warn you, some days ago when I say that before we finish this case, you will be angry, perhaps. More than that I cannot say, but now one can explain.

"You are a man of honour and you reveal nothing that I confide to you, and it was not of that that I was afraid. But it was possible that you should reveal something without knowing it, since you trusted implicitly this Henri Larne. There is a gesture perhaps, a look of the eyes, the answer to a question which apparently is nothing—all those would reveal to Henri Larne, and therefore to his brother, what I wish to conceal.

"You are still mystified? Then consider, my friend, that already you had begun to assure me that Henri Larne knew about his brother things which he did not wish to reveal. To myself I was forced to say that perhaps the brothers had some understanding, and I remember that if Pierre Larne knew of your hotel, and of the association between yourself and Braque, then it was only Henri who could have given the information. But you forgive these descriptions that I make on you?"

"I think you were absolutely justified," Travers said. "Undoubtedly I should have inadvertently put Henri Larne on his guard."

Gallois got solemnly to his feet.

"Observe this generosity," he said in a slow, spacious English which Charles might understand. "A colleague whom I deceive, but a colleague so perfect, so magnanimous, that he accepts at once the explanations which I so badly make."

His long arm reached out and he was shaking Travers once more by the hand.

"What I'm anxious to hear about," said the self-conscious Travers, "is not myself but that Fécamp business. As far as I'm concerned, it's still a muddle."

"To that we arrive," Gallois announced. "But first, we return to the night of the murder, where we agree that you have been brought to the flat of Braque in order that you may prove that it is at a quarter to six that he dies. And the assassin wishes that you prove this, because it is at a quarter to six that he has the alibi that is perfect. But there is something else that then occurs to me. If it is you who prove that Braque is dead at a quarter to six, then perhaps the assassin makes use of you also *to prove his own alibi!* And whose is the alibi that you, my friend, can prove? It is the alibi of Henri Larne. Once more, then, he comes in suspicion."

He raised a warning finger.

"But not as the assassin of Braque. That was impossible. But then you commence to tell me other things: that Henri Larne can give also an alibi for Pierre, and again I wonder. This Henri commences to be a person of importance in the case, and he is a mystery. Why should he refuse information about Pierre, who is a parasite? I say to myself that perhaps there is much pretence and that there is even the possibility that they work together to deceive the law.

"And so I explain about Fécamp, which to you now becomes simple. This Pierre departs in the car with those who are the Gurlots, as we think, but we lose the car. Then at last I hear that a car which resembles it is seen in the late afternoon as it passes through Fécamp, and then I hear no more. But I am unquiet and then I remember my suspicions of Henri Larne, and I arrange to go with you to his hotel. He is astonished that his brother is not on the way to Grenoble and he says at last that he will accompany us to confront this so treacherous brother. But he wishes a wait of half an hour and at once I know why.

"For I arrange already that one listens to the telephone, because if what I suspicion is right, then it is necessary that he warn this Pierre. And I am right! He rings a number at Fécamp, and he says a something which is not sense but which is doubtless a signal. This number that be rings is sent to the authorities at Fécamp, so that they verify, but the half-hour is already over and we must depart. So it is at Rouen that I learn that one has traced the number and I instruct that François watches the house. Then later on our journey I leave the car and I telephone again and one tells me precisely where one finds this house."

Travers had been bursting to say something, and now he got his question in.

"So that was why you pretended the wire of the telephone had been cut as early as dusk?"

"Precisely. I must assure Henri Larne that I am a fool, and it is essential also that he does not suspect that I think that it is he who has warned Pierre."

"And what actually happened at Fécamp, in that house?"

"At the moment I have not a certainty, but I think perhaps that it is this. When Pierre is warned, he announces that they must go to England in the motor-boat, and he abandons his own belongings. Moulins is carried to the boat and Pierre and the woman depart with him. But Pierre has contrived to make a hole in the boat, and at a certain moment he abandons the boat and returns to the shore in the dinghy, which has oars. The woman shrieks, perhaps, but who is to hear? In a minute the boat sinks and she is drowned, and Moulins also.

"But as he approaches the shore, Pierre observes the torch of François. So he abandons the small boat and makes a circle and attacks François. Then he takes the car and his belongings, and is gone.

"But even now, when I know that Henri has warned Pierre, what can I do? Henri has this alibi which proves that he himself did nothing. All I can do is to hope that we arrive at Pierre and force that he reveals what he knows. But one continues still to listen to the phone of Henri, and in the suite which adjoins his own I place a man who can both see and hear. This evening, by example, I know that you talk with him, and there is reported to me every word that you say. That, my friend, is why I seek you at the rue Vagnolles, where there is a picture of which you have talked much to Henri Larne.

"But we return. There was the death of Moulins and I discover who that he is, but I am an imbecile and I do not see that everything at once is changed, and that it is he who is of the importance. But this morning Henri Larne goes to Neuilly, and there he phones, and the call is traced. Pierre is found and he is followed to Paris, where one makes the arrest. But he protests that he has done nothing, and I imagine to myself that it is necessary to await the body of Hortense Gurlot. Then, my friend, when I am in this labyrinth, it is you who extricate me."

He was getting to his feet.

"And now what remains? That we celebrate this so happy conclusion? But to-morrow, perhaps, for to-night one must obtain the confession of these Larnes."

"Yes," said Travers. "To-morrow, perhaps, we might have some small celebration. But there's something else to do to-night."

Gallois looked surprised. Travers smiled.

"You, my friend, were the author and director of a certain comedy. One has played this comedy, But it is necessary that the curtain should descend with a grace, and that one should thank the actors."

Gallois spread his hands bewilderedly.

"But what is it you wish that I do?"

Travers nodded meaningly towards Charles.

"Perhaps it is in your private ear that I can best announce that. And perhaps also I was wrong. It is not the curtain that falls, but the last scene which we are about to play."

Gallois was still staring. Travers smiled as the door closed on Charles.

"A comedy, my dear Gallois, ends happily, and it is necessary that the audience should be happy also."

* * * * *

It was ten minutes before Charles returned, and now he was told to stand just away from the desk. A gendarme was at his elbow, and on the face of the supposed suspect was a look of patient misery, but his fingers twiddled nervously the cap which he held in his hand. Then Gallois ordered the woman Moulins to be brought in.

A quick look towards Charles, and she was approaching the desk. Gallois got to his feet.

"Elise Moulins, it is for the last time that you appear. The assassin of Braque has been apprehended. Regard the law henceforth, I beg of you, as your friend. That your affairs have been upset is regrettable, but there will be recompenses which doubtless will be made."

"Et mon frère?" she asked timidly.

Gallois looked down on her with eyes that had in them a pity and a sympathy that were profound.

"I myself will arrange that, as a friend."

He gave a little bow and resumed his seat.

"But there is another affair which remains. The accused, Charles Rabaud, is known to you?"

She nodded nervously, eyes once more full of fright.

"It is he who in your presence struck an *agent* that night in the rue Jourdoise, and then escaped?"

The eyes of Charles were patiently downcast. That snub nose of his gave a something pathetic to his misery, and there was once more that overwhelming resemblance to Gallois himself, Elise gave one quick look and then was shaking her head.

"It is not he."

Gallois stared in astonishment.

"Are you sure of it?"

"I am sure," she said. "It was not he."

Gallois let out a breath, stared bewilderedly· at Travers and got to his feet again. There he stood for a long while, and when at last his smile came, it came reluctantly.

"All that remains once more is to offer regrets. You can both depart."

"One moment," said Travers, and was rising suddenly from his chair. "There is a favour I demand of M. the Inspector I employ this Charles during my stay, but in a week the employment comes to an end. I want to inform you that he is of an exceptionally good character and of an unusual intelligence. But, unfortunately, I cannot take him to England."

"You suggest what, monsieur?"

"That he is one for whom the law might find a more permanent employment. It is I who recommend him. I assure you that he is the type that one would surely desire."

Gallois was shaking his head, and then all at once was shrugging his shoulders.

"Very well," he said, and not without amusement. "One makes mistakes and it is necessary to pay. And you, *mon garçon,* you have heard the admirable description that your employer gives. You desire, perhaps, to present yourself here tomorrow, so that one may examine and perhaps arrange?"

The eyes of Charles rose.

"Yes, monsieur, if it pleases you and *M. le patron.*"

"Leave, then, your particulars at the bureau," Gallois said, and waved the intimation to depart.

The door closed. Gallois was silent for a moment, then all at once he laughed! It was the laugh of a moment or two, but to Travers it was a tremendous event. But hardly before he could stare, Gallois was getting to his feet again.

"The curtain falls, then," he said, "and the audience departs happy."

"I must be departing too," Travers said, "or my wife will be worrying herself again."

"You permit that I arrange a car?"

"I don't know," Travers said. "There's a lot of things I'd like to think over. If it's a fine night I might walk after all."

He was drawing back the curtain to look at the weather, and then his eyes fell on the street below. Then something caught his puzzled attention.

"Come here a moment," he said to Gallois. "It rather looks to me as if the curtain has not fallen after all."

Across the street, Charles was waiting beneath a lamp-post. Gallois smiled at the sight of him, and the recalling of the last few minutes.

"It is you who commence to spoil him," he said. "It is not good to praise the young."

"And what of yourself?" Travers challenged him. "Don't you—"

His hand closed on Gallois' arm. A girl was running quickly across the road beneath them, and dodging a taxi, and reaching the lamp-post where Charles waited. He went a yard or two to meet her. They linked arms, and one could see all their excited happiness. Then they moved off along the pavement and were lost to sight. Travers let the curtain fall.

"*Voilà, mon ami.* The comedy is indeed played, but it is a romance that begins."

Gallois frowned for a moment, then the humour of things came back, and he was near to laughing again.

"When one is young," he said, and took Travers by the arm.

"Yes," said Travers. "When one is young. In those days perhaps you also had your affairs?"

"Perhaps—but one only," said Gallois slowly. "In this supreme moment of our friendship, it is something that I confess. But it was not a comedy. It commenced perhaps by what you call romance, and then—"

He shrugged his shoulders for the rest. Travers drew him to a halt by the door.

"And in this moment of our friendship, it is permitted that I ask a question?"

"There is nothing, my friend, that you cannot ask."

"Then this romance. There was perhaps a nose that was—*retroussé*?"

"With you and me, who have a friendship so exceptional, there are questions of which one divines already the answers."

For a moment there had been in his look some tragedy of remembrance, but now he was shrugging his shoulders, and in his eyes was all the old affection and something even of humour.

"As for this Charles, and this Elise, they live in the present. It is only the past that persists."

Once more his hand went out. Travers grasped it warmly, and in the brief moment he thought of many things. There was a morning in the Tate Gallery, the sprawling figure of the dead Braque, the white ghastliness of the face of Moulins, and all the embittered tragedy of Henri Larne. But it was of the lovers in the lamplight that he thought last.

"Yes," he said. "To them the present, and to you and me the past. And the best is still left. The future, my friend—for them and for us all."

THE END